Nicholas Torrens

# ONLOOKER

'Quick,' Peter said urgently. 'Quick.' He got up and began to move into the wood.

'No.'

'Come on.'

'No.'

'I'll leave you here,' Peter threatened. 'I'll go by myself. This is what we came for; no wonder there are stories about this place. Get up!' He pulled Isobel to her feet. 'Don't turn your torch on. We won't be caught if we're careful.'

'Caught? ' The word froze Isobel again, but to keep her balance she had to go where Peter pulled her. They moved almost silently, feeling their way among the giant trees. It seemed to Isobel that the wood had grown still bigger in the darkness: they inched onwards for what felt like whole minutes. Then Peter tightened his grip on her arm. They stopped.

# ONLOOKER

*Roger Davenport*

RED FOX

A Red Fox Book
Published by Arrow Books Limited
20 Vauxhall Bridge Road, London SW1V 2SA
An imprint of The Random Century Group

London Melbourne Sydney Auckland
Johannesburg and agencies throughout the world

First published by The Bodley Head 1989
Red Fox edition 1990



Set in Sabon
by JH Graphics Ltd, Reading

Made and printed in Great Britain
by Courier International, Tiptree, Essex

ISBN 0 09 975070 8

*For Alexandra*

Of the many books that were of help in writing this book, I found especially useful *A History of Kent* by Frank W. Jessup, and *British Society and the French Wars 1793–1815* by Clive Emsley

# One

'Invasion!'

'What?'

Mr Ford lowered the paper an inch or so and looked at his son across the kitchen table. 'It's only a headline. I wish I had a pound for every time they mention the Channel Tunnel.'

'Oh, that.' Peter poured the last of the milk on to his cereal and started to mash it into a pale brown cement.

'Enough milk, is there?' His mother was drinking her tea black, he noticed. In the sunshine her hair was a halo of untidiness and her look of anxiety, as always, touched Peter.

'Yes thanks,' he lied.

'And I wish I had a penny for every traveller who ever came through Kent.'

'You'd be the world's richest man,' Peter answered his father. 'It's always been the way into England.'

'Another record for tourists this year, they reckon. Can't call the country your own these days.'

'I expect that's what the Saxons said about the Danes.'

Mr Ford turned a page of his paper. 'Your bike mended then, old boy?'

'Mmm.'

'Well done, old chap.' It sometimes seemed Peter's father wanted to give the impression he had a public school or army background. *Not officer material.* The phrase came unworthily into Peter's mind and he only half rejected it. The cereal looked unappealing.

'Where's my homework?'

'In the front room where you left it.' His mother had begun to put grips in her hair, at random.

'I'm off, then.'

'Not zero hour, is it? Aren't you going to help your mother with the washing-up?'

'I did it last night, didn't I? I'm going the long way.'

'It's a lovely morning,' his mother said. 'I'm sorry about the milk, love.'

Outside it was colder than it had appeared to be. Peter slipped over his shoulders the rucksack that held his school work and gym things and went down the narrow garden to the shed where he kept his bike. Next door, in the other of the pair of grey brick houses, he could hear Mr Williams making excuses to his wife about the time at which he had returned last night. All round, a normal start to a normal day.

In the heart of the village Peter took a racing turn down the lane which led to the Saxon way, causing an oncoming car to brake hard, quite unnecessarily, in Peter's opinion. Now the old trees closed in above him and the pedals whipped round as the ancient, gearless bike clattered downhill, its front fork vibrating loosely. The bend: lean into it, the cowslip in the verge tapping at his shoulder then the road levelled out and Peter let the bicycle dictate its own sedate pace. Above him and to his left, a steep green bank; to his right, trees, and through them . . . the English Channel. Of course, there were the fields of the Romney Marsh between him and the Channel, but at this height and angle there was only the distant water. Peter looked at his watch. Had he time to take the 'longer' long way? Through the trees he saw the tiny shape of an old coaster or freighter out in the Channel, appearing otionless as the trees slid by. Ahead of him and to the right, a path to the edge of the cliffs . . . to the left, as the bank gradually lowered itself, a dull road through fields, and school. He turned left.

A tennis ball rattled in the spokes of his front wheels as he coasted through the morning kick-about and freewheeled into the cool twilight of the bike shed. Patel was examining the handlebars of his new racer.

'Screwed the bell on too tight. Rust. That's all I need.'

'I've got plenty, if you want some.'

'Ha,ha. Amazing – I didn't know you could get rust on a heap of old lead.'

'What are you doing at the weekend?'

'Trip to France.' Patel sounded gloomy. Frequent excursions to the Boulogne hypermarket had lost whatever glamour they had once possessed. 'What are you doing?'

'Whatever I like.'

The bell was sounding as Peter avoided two second-formers, a boy and a girl who were scuffling and giggling over a fallen satchel, and wandered into the boys' lavatory.

Alone there, he wet his hair and slowly combed it in front of the mirror. His broad-featured face regarded him placidly. It was, he had decided, a face suited to the great outdoors and whatever the elements could throw at it. He attempted a quietly shrewd gaze and achieved only a look of smug cunning. He sighed. The bell had stopped ringing – for how long?

'Hurry up, hurry up, Ford. It may be only thirty seconds to you but if you multiply that thirty seconds by the number of people you're keeping waiting you'll find you've wasted nearly a quarter of an hour of our collective time . . . No, Peter – not unless you want to sit on someone's lap . . .'

Laughter, particularly from the girls, who forced it. Peter blushed. He had been making for his accustomed desk at the back, which he now saw was occupied by Barry Leadbetter. Barry's often proclaimed view was that girls, were more interesting than football. Evidently he had today fixed his sights on Annette Waring, who sat in front of him already clearly nervous.

'At the front, Peter, which for your information is that section of the room nearest to me . . . ' Less laughter this time and Mr Jarvis, Geography, continued his patter smoothly, appearing hardly to have paused at all for further appreciation ' . . . You are sitting next to Isobel Stanton, whom I've just introduced to the class. You can make your own introductions at a later date, after we've had a brief foray into Scandinavia. *Now*. Climate – as we know – is a contributory factor in any society . . .'

Jarvis rattled on. Peter sat down next to the new girl. Had he heard anything about this? He looked at her, a dark-complexioned girl wearing an expensive cream pullover. Her eyes were deep green and unfriendly. At thirteen or so she was probably slightly younger than Peter, who refused to respond to her combative glance.

* * *

'What's the word on the new girl, Pat?'

Patel rubbed the top of the lemonade can with a dark thumb and passed it over to Peter. They were leaning against the main gate, looking inward at four sixth- formers who were conducting a private anti-smoking campaign by a stop-and-search procedure. The lunch break was almost at an end.

'Dad's an archaeologist. They're renting a place outside Folkestone. Paying too much for it. She's got no mum.'

'Dead?'

'Dead, divorced – what's the difference?' Patel's father had a shop in Hythe. His son affected a cynical exterior but was too enthusiastic at his studies for anyone to take him seriously as a hard man. He was always well informed and Peter regarded him as being as close to a best friend as he had.

'What's she doing here?' Peter asked.

'Putting on an act, if you ask me. She spent a long time in the toilet in first break.' Patel scrunched up the can and they ambled back towards the main building. Dark clouds were forming and the school became ugly in the open countryside, its windows tall and blank, staring out over the grey asphalt of the recreation areas.

'Why does she have to sit next to me? That's all I ask.'

'Because you're a White Anglo Saxon Protestant with a friendly face.'

'More'n she's got.'

Peter decided to be friendly. 'See you tomorrow, then.'

'Yes.' Isobel gave Peter a tight smile.

'It's all right here, when you get used to it.'

'Yes.'

'How are you getting home?'

'Daddy's got a car.'

'Ah . . . Well . . . See you tomorrow.'

Isobel watched Peter lope over to the bike shed, passing through groups of children who did not in any way acknowledge him. He was strange, she thought. Relaxed and open and yet . . . a real loner. Someone who didn't need people. Like her, she didn't need people. Not these days. With a sharp twinge of embarrassment, she saw her father walking towards her – the only adult in view. His voice was loud, too, as he neared her.

'Well! How was it?'

'OK.'

Professor Stanton put his hand on Isobel's shoulder as they walked out of the school. He was a tall man and Isobel found this form of physical contact patronizing. He was so sure of himself, of his intelligence, his balanced attitude, his wry view of people and places.

'You know, Isobel, when they built this place they may well have concreted over something fascinating. A Saxon burial ground. A Roman camp. Kent is the most exciting county – the gateway to Britain for invaders since – well – since when?'

Isobel recognized his 'history made interesting for the young' tone, and walked on steadily, looking at no one. She was pleased they had the new car, the Range Rover. Her father had never been very interested in appearances and she felt she had to coax him to make the best of himself since . . . She wondered whether the money for the Range Rover had come from an insurance policy on her mother's life. That had not occurred to her before. But of course they were well-off anyway . . . She'd never know. One couldn't ask about a thing like that.

Professor Stanton did not yet know the area well, so they sped to the new house along main roads. The new house. The hired house. Nothing would ever have any permanence again, certainly not enough to put your trust in.

'How long are we going to be here, Daddy?'

'How long is a piece of string? I don't know. It depends how the work goes. It depends on a lot of things. The school's all right, isn't it? You're very quiet.'

'It's OK.'

'I don't suppose you'll be there long, anyway. We must make proper plans. Anyone nice in your class?'

'Don't be stupid. How would I know?'

'Yes. Early days.'

Isobel shifted in the large seat. The windscreen was picking up the first drops of rain, but the Professor did not use the wipers yet. The drops of rain started to merge, trembling as they clung to their hold on the screen.

'Daddy . . .'

'Yes.'

'Do you think if Mummy was alive she'd want us to move from London?'

'Do you mean would she want *you* to move from London?'

'I don't think she would. She loved London. So do I.'

'No one likes change in their lives. You know, Isobel, you assume a lot on your mother's behalf sometimes.'

'What do you mean?'

'You make judgements for her. Ones we can never

know about, now. You want to stay in London – all right, tell me about that – don't tell me it's Mummy I'm going to upset.'

'You forget quickly, don't you?'

'That's unfair, Bella.'

They drove on in silence.

Outside Lympne, Peter and Patel split up. In the dingy, wet light, Patel's silver bomber jacket seemed to give off a fluorescent glow as he accelerated away round the bend and down in the dirction of Hythe. He called something over his shoulder, but it was lost in the increasing rain.

Peter was now committed to the 'longer' long way home and water was running down his neck and penetrating his torn track shoes. He took the bicycle down the lane that led off the main road, standing on the pedals to work up momentum. A cracking noise coincided with a pedal slipping sharply and he knew the chain had come off. The useless pedal had scraped his calf, which was painful. He began to feel distinctly cross.

Dismounting, he looked around for shelter. Sheep stood in a field, the lambs pressed tight against the ewes. In the middle of the field was a bowed sheet of corrugated iron of a height to accommodate damp sheep. Peter carried the old bicycle to the ditch by the road and used it as a stile by which to climbed over the barbed wire fence. Then, leaving the bicycle to its deserved solitude, he trudged through the thick, soaking grass to the sheep shelter. The sheep seemed uninhibited by the steady rain and took sprightly evasive action as he passed among them. There was only one dank, woolly inhabitant of the shelter and this became entirely undignified in its scramble to vacate the premises. Peter bent double and entered the dark, warm-smelling shelter.

He lay on his belly watching the grass outside shifting in waves of rain, and very soon began to feel comfortable. There were strands of wool caught in the rusty corrugated iron, and he twisted one of these in his fingers, feeling the coarse individual hairs through the covering of greasy lanolin. He started to plait the wool, working slowly but with a skill that surprised him.

A break in the clouds sent light racing across the field. The rain was settling into a series of showers. Peter squirmed out of the shelter reluctantly, aware that dirty as he now was, it wasn't worth risking further parental anger by being too late home. He stretched, and the wind carried his hair over his eyes. He flicked his head round to free his vision and saw that, on the horizon, on the far brow of a neighbouring field, the rain had not stopped farm work. Two horses were pulling a long plough, appearing to have as their captive the man who stumbled through the heavy earth after them, wrestling the plough to his will. It looked a tiring and dispiriting business, set harshly against the leaden sky.

Peter turned and ran at the nearby sheep, who panicked in a satisfactory fashion. He was thinking that the good thing about having a bike like his was that nobody in their right mind would want to steal it. Mind you, he'd swap with Patel any day . . . Perhaps he should take a few links out of the chain; it came off often enough to qualify as a serious health hazard. He found his injured calf was causing him to limp and pulled up at the fence breathing heavily. He looked back. The plough, horses and man had disappeared, presumably working the continuation of the field over the hill. But a horse-drawn plough? Ploughing what, exactly? And in early May? That was curious. Still, perhaps it was one of those 'organic' farms, ploughing in manure. Anyway it was probably lucky he hadn't been spotted. He climbed back over the fence and set his slippery fingers the task of replacing the bicycle chain on its teeth.

Some minutes later he passed the beech trees of Culver Wood, sorry he had no time to stop off. Recently the 'longer' long way had become the usual way to and from school, and Peter had a growing feeling it was the wood that was the chief attraction of this route. If you penetrated to its extremities there was a sheer drop down to the farming land of the Romney Marsh; land which appeared to be rolled out flat so that the Channel beyond could at any moment surge back over the fields right to the foot of the inland cliff on which the wood stood. Perhaps he and Patel could camp out there one night, looking down at the far-off lights of Hythe and the further glow of Folkestone. But he'd be there alone, he suddenly knew. It was not a place to be shared. He stood cautiously on the pedals and Culver Wood vanished behind him for another day.

'I've run a bath for you. I knew you'd be wet,' Mrs Ford said, ignoring Peter with a resolution that expressed anger or disappointment in him. His mother looked tired and one side of her face was smudged blue. The kitchen was steamy and on the electric hob a large covered saucepan continued to fill the room with pungent vapour. Any garment bought by Mrs Ford was continually altered in shape or colour until its old age could no longer be denied and sometimes an irresistibly inexpensive buy would undergo immediate transformation. Once Peter had imagined she shop-lifted clothes and was then compelled to disguise them. He hoped that whatever was changing colour in the pan was not his.

'Hurry up. It'll be cold already and there's no more hot water except for your father.'

Her refusal to be cross with him moved Peter to lie. 'I stayed behind at school. There's a new girl in class. Her dad was late picking her up.'

A spark of warmth lit Mrs Ford's face. 'And you stayed behind with her? That was nice.'

'Yes. Her father's an archaeologist.' The circumstantial detail added substance to the lie, Peter thought.

'And you're going to be friends, are you?'

Now the lie was regretted. 'I don't know. Where's Dad?'

'I don't know, dear.'

Mr Ford arrived in a self-important way while they were eating. The dish was one Mrs Ford called 'Californian', consisting of mince and tinned sweetcorn. Peter's father waved it away. 'No, no. I've eaten. All well here?' He asked the question as a courtesy, his belief was that problems were something that happened only to working men.

'What sort of a day have you had?' Mrs Ford asked.

'Busy. Busy. I've been making . . .'

'Headway?'

A favourite word, but wrong this evening. 'Contacts. Actually I *will* have some of that, if there's any going.'

He looked tired himself, then. Since being made redundant as area manager for a tyre company, his efforts to remain employed had never borne fruit for long. He was now a salesman for a motor-mower concern, recently 'appointed', as he put it.

'Peter made a new friend at school today.'

'Did you? Well done.'

'Her father's an archaeologist,' Mrs Ford added.

'Clever chap, then. After all, the future of this country is all behind it!' Mr Ford laughed at his own joke, eating rapidly. 'No, seriously, the past is a great industry. Better than a lot of the newer ones, at any rate . . . You're good at history, aren't you Peter? You'll have a lot in common, then.'

Peter could see his father's mind, a demented mountain goat, leaping from one castle in the air to another with practised ease.

'I just talked to this girl, that's all.' Unspoken: *We are not about to get married and nor am I about to become her father's assistant.*

Mrs Ford did not take the hint. 'What's he like?'

'Who?'

'This man – the girl's father. You waited for him.'

'Oh, he's . . . very . . . polite.' Not even having seen Mr Stanton, Peter felt safe with this description.

'Seriously though, old chap, you could do a lot worse than becoming an archaeologist. Think about it.'

Careers. How did anyone come to a decision when they were always being pushed and prodded?

'Yes – I might.'

Careers.

'What does your father do?'

'He works in machinery.' Peter refused to say 'salesman' having been born as the son of an 'area manager'.

'What sort of machinery?'

'Garden machinery.'

'Garden machinery like . . .?'
'Like machines you use in gardens.'
'Like sprinklers, you mean? Does he make them?'
'No.'
'Does he sell them, then?'
Peter gave up and grinned. 'Not often. And they're lawn mowers.'
Isobel only just managed to keep from smiling back at him. The weather had abruptly changed. They sat, feet out in front of them, with their backs against the warm wall of one of the pre-fab classrooms. Weeds were already forcing their way through the concrete base of the building.
Isobel was tenacious, Peter had discovered, and, having decided to honour him with her conversation, would not be put off. For her part, Isobel had started out looking for a chance to complain about the school and anything else that occurred to her, but Peter's character was too relaxed to allow spite to blossom for long.
'My father says he's a salesman, too.'
'I thought he was an archaeologist.'
'Yes, but to raise money you've got to be able to sell yourself *and* your business – whatever it is – he says. That's how he got the money to do what he's doing now.'
'Yes?'
'He's got money from big companies. It's a tax loss for them, or good public relations, or something.'
'Oh yes?'
'There's a place called Culver Wood. He's starting there.'
Peter looked at her. 'Starting what?'
'A dig. You know, grubbing about for old broken things under the ground.'

Peter felt unaccountably disturbed. 'Isn't it private property?'

'I don't know. He's got permission, anyway.'

Peter got to his feet.

'What's the matter?'

No answer came to him. He took off one of his track shoes and shook it. Nothing came out.

'I scraped my leg yesterday.'

'Did you? Go on, show us.'

He put the shoe back on and smiled at her, and this time Isobel could not help smiling back. He looked older and indefinably more confident when he smiled – he was almost charming, she found herself thinking. He walked away, the undone laces trailing.

It was almost dark in Culver Wood, although today the brightness outside filtered through here and there in uneven, changing patterns, softened by the surrounding green of the fresh beech leaves. Peter walked farther in, taking deep, steady breaths as he let the old, still atmosphere seep down into him. To be here he had biked away from school at a pace even Patel might have admired. Would he go to look out over the Channel, or . . .?

He arrived at his favourite spot, a small clearing somewhere near the centre of the wood. Here, light slanted down in seemingly solid shafts. Nearby, one of the roots of a tree rose in a snake-like configuration before clawing into the ground. Sometimes he would perch on it, sitting quietly for minutes at an end. Today he broke the cathedral atmosphere of the wood as he said aloud, 'What's Mr Stanton looking for?' He squatted down and scraped his hands through the earth. 'What is it he's looking for?' He let the loose earth fall from his fingers and began to dig at the ground in earnest, as though he were a dog after a buried treat. Twigs, the skeletons of leaves, earth. 'There's nothing *here*.' He rose to his feet and touched the strong green bark of a tree. It felt like iron: permanent. He wiped his dirty hands on it and turned to walk away and stopped.

Standing not six metres from him was a man. A short, hook-nosed man of indeterminate age, wearing an old tweed hat above a dark pullover and nondescript trousers. The total effect was of an entirely unremarkable being, except for the deep-set, watchful eyes which were now fixed on Peter with an almost hypnotic stillness. Perhaps it was a gamekeeper . . . or someone to do with Isobel's father. Instinctively, Peter was apologetic.

'I'm sorry. I'm just going.'

The man stepped back, saying nothing. Peter did not look at him as he walked past. Now he felt angry. Probably the man had no more right to be there than he had. Less, probably. Perhaps he was an American tourist – the season for them had begun – but he hadn't been carrying a camera. Still, he could be a foreigner, which was why he hadn't spoken.

Riding home, Peter identified the cause of an anxiety that was nagging at him. The man had seemed familiar. What the association might be, Peter could not establish. He was sure only that it was not a pleasant one.

# Two

Isobel gave the solid rubber ball another lunging whack and it raced away off the racquet-shaped piece of wood she held, before charging back just as eagerly, a prisoner on a length of strong elastic. She stepped around the metal stake anchoring the elastic to the lawn and played a clumsy imitation of a forehand volley, which bent her wrist as the ball slammed on to the edge of the bat and dropped to the ground. She picked the ball up and played her next shot towards the house, timing it sweetly so that the ball made every effort to shatter the window of her father's study before being drawn back by the pull of the elastic. Isobel stooped to play a backhand and the ball cannoned off the bat and on to her chin. She sat down on the lush grass of the lawn, more cross than hurt.

What her father wanted, of course, was for her to develop a sudden passion for tennis – or any game, anything that would involve her with other people of her own age. She saw through him so easily. 'Records or tapes – that's all – or books,' she had responded when he had announced his intention of getting her 'some things for the country'. But he thought she was too much alone and as usual went his own way, buying her a new bicycle, the practice-tennis set and a tent which could apparently accommodate a family of four. 'You can have some friends round – camp on the lawn, if you like. I used to love that.' To which her reply should have been, 'Well you do it, then.'

Reluctantly, she had to admit the house was attractive. She slumped into a dejected attitude, which she hoped her father would notice if he happened to look out of the window. Some chance of that . . . he was 'busy right now, darling.' No, the house was all right, in a countrified sort of way. Low-built, of warm brick beneath the white wooden weatherboard of the first floor, it looked irritatingly comfortable. Her room was nice, too. But it wasn't *theirs*, its welcoming security belonged to someone else. It smelt new inside, redecorated to be let to strangers, her father and herself, people passing through.

A rattling noise made her lift her head; her father was struggling with the study window, which, swollen by a coat of fresh paint, did not open as it should. He made a comical face, pretending terror, and waving his arms sank from sight like a drowning man. Isobel waited. He reappeared and opened the window with a sharp blow of his fist, smiling the while to show nothing could make him angry.

'Do you want to give Mrs Davies a hand with the washing?'

Isobel stayed where she was. 'I thought you'd never ask.'

'Just a thought. It'd be a friendly gesture. Hey – come here – I want to talk to you.' Isobel rose and walked to the window, holding the plywood bat as though reluctant to leave her game.

'No, silly – inside. Come and have a look.' Isobel obeyed and wandered slowly round to the back door, smiling briefly at Mrs Davies, who was unloading washing from the machine in the kitchen. In the hall, familiar pictures looked alien in their new surroundings.

The crates in the Professor's study had been emptied and, for a second, looking around her, a picture of his old study in Islington flashed into Isobel's mind. The room here was larger, but her father had arranged his things in the same relative positions as in the old house. The leather-topped desk in the centre of the room; trestle tables, bare as yet, right across the back wall; the two brightly painted wooden statues on either side of the window. Isobel felt a pang of love for her father, who had so obviously tried to recreate the room he had left in the house they had moved from. The Professor's good humour indicated no self pity, however.

'Now we're getting somewhere, eh? What you need are some posters and stuff for your room. We'll have a go at that next week, if you like.'

'Good idea. You've certainly done great here, Daddy,' Isobel approved, wanting to please.

'That's what I've done, is it? I've "done great" . . . Well, it'll do when the room's cleared. Now look here.' He took her hand in his and spoke with exaggerated slowness. 'What . . . are . . . we . . . going . . . to do . . . today?' He looked at her triumphantly, and with a sinking heart she realized he had a treat in store for her.

'I . . . don't . . . know,' she answered patiently.

'I mean, it's some time till tea-time, so – well, we could go somewhere.'

'Like where?'

'We could have tea out, if you like – no reason why not?'

'Where?' Already they had been together to local places her father thought would interest her almost as much as him: the ruins of Stutfall Castle, where to her dismay they had spent more time than in the more recent and appealing Lympne Castle, which overlooked its Roman predecessor on the old Saxon Cliff; to the zoo park at Port Lympne – which she *had* enjoyed – and to the quite exceptionally dull Roman fort of Reculver. 'I suppose you want to go back to that Roman fort,' she said, in a depressed voice.

'No, of course not,' said her father equably, 'since you didn't have the sense to appreciate it. I had in mind the Butterfly Centre.'

'What happens there?'

'They have butterflies.'

'What do the butterflies do?'

'They feed, they breed, they flutter about.'

'Where is it?'

'Not far.'

'Do you mind if I don't?'

Professor Stanton consciously made his response sound mild. 'Well, I'm not going by myself – *you* think of something we can do.'

'Actually, looking at all this, I think I'll give my room a going over.'

Her father brightened. 'Good thinking. Smashing.'

Upstairs, in the clean white room overlooking the small orchard at the back of the house, Isobel lay on her bed and stared at the ceiling. The smell of new paint lingered here, too, reminding her somehow of a hospital.

*It is a contradictory image of great power,* the Professor wrote. *Mithras, the great Lord of Light, is a man hewn from the living rock, a weighty creature of stone who at the end of his term on earth is borne up to heaven on a ray of light, in the sun's chariot . . . To the Roman legionnaire, perhaps far from home, the worship of Mithras was—*

The Professor paused, disconsolate. When attempting to interest others in his pet subject he all too frequently lost interest himself. He looked at the life-sized wooden statues flanking the window. The two replicated attendants of Mithras looked back at him sidelong, Cautes with his upturned torch representing hope, and Cautopates, whose torch was turned down. Since Helen Stanton's death after a long illness, the despondent Cautopates had been in the ascendant in the Professor's life. He read over what he had written. If he had any sense he would be manufacturing coffee tables, he thought, not writing books to put on them. Sitting back in his chair he gazed again at the statues. They did look remarkably good where they were placed, facing inwards, heads slightly to one side, guarding the window as they had in Islington . . . No, not guarding – here quite obviously waiting. Waiting for the god sprung from stone to return from the heavens, perhaps borne on a shaft of light like that which now picked out the metal binders on one of the packing cases. The packing cases. Really he should stack those away in the garage before he did any more work. The Professor stood up with relief, letting the biro fall.

'She's crazy, bringing her pump to school. You'd better tell her.'

'Why me?'

Patel said, 'Because you're her friend.'

'I'm not.'

'Well *I'm* not. I think she's prejudiced – you know?'

'Oh no,' Peter let his envious attention leave the

immaculate, gleaming bicycle on which Isobel had arrived that day. 'She's like she is with you with everyone. She doesn't want to know.'

Final break was ending. They started to saunter back from the bike shed to the main building. 'She wants to know *you*,' Patel said with half-hearted malice.

'Don't be daft. We sit together in class, that's all.'

'Yes – every class . . .'

'Well, people do, don't they? It wasn't my idea.' Peter felt uncomfortable. Isobel and her father had been on his mind over the weekend. They didn't belong here, that was the essence of it. He, of course, did belong. His family had lived here for generations. And even the Patels belonged, because they had settled here with nowhere else to go and were working to make a life for themselves, taking an interest in local affairs, and so on. But the Stantons, they were like the tourists who invaded the county in the summer, foreigners wherever they had come from, even if it was only London. Yet the Professor was here with a purpose . . .

As they entered the school Peter said, 'Why do people want to muck about in the past – like this Professor Stanton?' He saw Isobel then, almost at his shoulder as a group caught up with him and Patel, about to go into the classroom. Isobel's glance at him expressed no anger, but he found himself blushing.

'Probably because it's interesting and it pays,' said the pragmatic Patel, unaware of Isobel until she pushed past them, aloof. 'Whoops.'

The class was relaxed and bored, waiting for the entrance of Mr Seltman, History. He was an enthusiast in everything he did, which was why he was late and why he would doubtless outstay his welcome when he arrived, continuing after the last bell of the day. Peter sat down beside Isobel, who ignored him. He ignored her right back.

'Buzz off, Jack. You can take my place. On your bike – go on.' Peter looked round to see Barry Leadbetter moving into the desk behind Isobel, his large hands grasping Jack Bennett's collar as though he were a bouncer in a nightclub. Appropriately for his mission in life, Barry appeared to be all eyes and lips. Peter looked beyond him to the back of the class, where Annette Waring was whispering to a friend. She saw him and shrugged and grinned, evidently relieved Barry had transferred his attentions elsewhere.

Leadbetter said in a carrying voice: 'Talking of bikes, you've got a nice one.'

His attention was on Isobel's back. She half turned. 'Talking to me?'

Barry smiled and ran a hand through his wavy black hair. 'Oh, yes.' Having got her attention he favoured the silent stare approach. It worked, in that Isobel again faced front, looking ruffled.

Someone's paper dart rapped against a window and a fight ensued over it; the noise level was muted, no one was in the mood for trouble so close to the end of the day. Peter saw Isobel straighten in her chair and he looked round again. Leadbetter had a ruler pressed into her back as though he was taking her hostage, using a knife.

'You know what – as well as a nice bike, you've got a nice *back*.'

As far as Peter understood the Leadbetter method of courtship, it involved a period of unsettling tactics followed by a suddenly protective, caring attitude that cut out from the herd the animal he was after. It was not that Peter had any great objection to Barry's games – he simply didn't want them going on around *him*. He turned fully in his seat, resting his elbow on the back of the chair.

'Do you want a little bit of trouble, Barry?'

'What?'

'That's what you're going to get if you don't pack it in.'

'Come off it.'

'I mean it.'

Barry did not mind fighting if there was good reason for it, and was more than willing if he could be certain of a home win. In this case it was by no means a sure thing. He withdrew the ruler.

'I didn't know you cared. Soft on her, are you?' He smiled and Peter smiled back with genuine anger. His expression decided Barry. He leaned forward to Isobel.

'Well, if you get tired of him just let me know, will you?' He sat back not displeased with his performance, then nodded to the door, 'Man on'.

The football phrase referred to the whirlwind entry of Mr Seltman, who almost at once began talking rapidly.

'Economics. War. Bread. Who said "an army marches on its stomach"? Anyone?'

From the back, 'Nelson?'

'No. Why would he say that? He was a sailor last I heard. Napoleon. It's attributed to Napoleon. Right, here we are in the Napoleonic wars of the late seventeenth and early eighteenth centuries, we men of Kent, up against it with our backs to the wall. "In Britain",' he declaimed, in his light, nasal voice, ' "Is one breath; We all are with you now from shore to shore; Ye men of Kent, 'tis victory or death!" Wordsworth. Why did he refer so specifically to Kent? Because, as ever, it was the county of England most immediately under threat of invasion. Being so close to the continent. Now, the men of Kent are listening to Napoleon, who's saying that with three days' east wind he could repeat the exploits of William the Conqueror. And they're no fools, they know it's not an empty threat, but they've other things on their minds, too. Everyday things. Life goes on even in wartime. What were they thinking about?'

'Who's going to win the league?' (Leadbetter).

'Find out for me when the Football League was started and tell me by lunchtime tomorrow or you're for it, mate. All right? All right. They were worried about their stomachs. War tends to bring full employment but – as witness rationing in the Second World War – filling your stomach can be a problem, particularly if you're a farm labourer paid only around two and six a week – that's twelve and a half pence. They're having poor harvests and the price of wheat is high. How much did a loaf of bread cost? Anyone? Have a guess. Say it's 1803, how much is bread?'

There was a dull silence, weighted with lack of interest from the class. Peter took pity on Mr Seltman.

'Around a shilling?'

'Old money?' Mr Seltman asked quickly.

'Oh, . . . old. Yes – old money.'

'Double it and you're nearer the mark. Two shillings for a quartern loaf of bread. Nearly a week's wages for some working men. Of course there was home baking in those days, but –'

'No!' Peter surprised himself by speaking. Mr Seltman's breezy manner didn't normally exasperate him as it did today. The word had shot out with some vehemence.

'What do you mean, "No"? How else do you think people managed?'

'No. The price of bread. It wasn't two shillings.'

'Well, I can assure you it was.'

'Not round here.'

'No doubt it varied from area to area, but it undoubtedly cost about the same amount of money as a farm labourer earned in a week.' This was obviously the equation that appealed to Mr Seltman.

'That's not true.' The class began to pay attention. Isobel looked at Peter. He was red in the face and looked stubborn.

'Are you looking for a pointless argument, Ford?'

'No.' Peter spoke slowly, trying to contain his anger. 'It's just not as pat as you make it sound.'

'Pat? That's butter, isn't it? A pat of butter? And how much was *butter* – round here, of course!' Mr Seltman spoke with heavy sarcasm, as though he had been taking tips from Mr Jarvis, Geography.

'Don't be a fool!' Peter snapped, then controlled himself. 'You wanted to know what the price of bread was, so . . . so I . . .' He tailed off, all at once bewildered. What did he know about it, anyway? This was ridiculous. Mr Seltman took advantage of his uncertainty.

'I wanted to *tell* you so that you might learn. That's what I'm here for. See me after.'

Peter's whole body was alive with humiliation. He looked at the desk, anywhere but at Isobel who was regarding him with concern. Mr Seltman was red in the face, too.

'Anyone else want to waste our time? Right. We'll continue. One of my purposes is to show how attractive the lure of the army might be to certain members of the populace. The navy, of course, is another case . . .' Mr Seltman regained his verve and began chalking on the blackboard. 'NO COMPULSORY MILITARY SERVICE AS SUCH.'

Peter sat alone in the tall classroom. As whenever a crowd has left a space, the objects in the classroom took on an added stillness: desks, chairs, the wall-charts, the lights hanging halfway down from the ceiling, reflecting rather than giving light in the mid-afternoon, all made their inanimate presence felt. Mr Seltman had left the class with the others without speaking to Peter. Perhaps he wouldn't come back; no matter, sitting here idly was by no means unpleasant.

'Right then, lad. Fever over, is it?'

Mr Seltman was back, carrying the PVC briefcase that accompanied his arrival and departure from the school.

'I beg your pardon?' Peter said politely.

'I can see it is.' Mr Seltman cocked his head to one side and looked curiously at Peter, his pale eyes not unfriendly. 'You were in quite a state back there.'

'Was I?' Peter was surprised. It all seemed a long time ago.

'Yes. Mind you – perhaps I shouldn't have been so dogmatic myself!' Mr Seltman said cheerily. 'After all – local prices in different areas . . . at certain times of year – well, prices do vary, don't they? Now, I've been honest with you, so you be honest with me. You were just guessing – right?'

Peter got up, disliking the interrogation. 'Well no . . . I don't know . . . I don't think so.'

'You read it somewhere?'

'Read it, or saw it on the telly . . . I don't know.'

The teacher seized on the idea as being the obvious explanation. 'Ah yes. Yes . . . It's usually the telly, isn't it. There's so much information coming our way from that damn machine, it's a wonder our brains don't burst.'

'Yes. I suppose it must have been the telly.'

'Well, it doesn't matter.' Mr Seltman dropped the subject, but he had not finished with Peter. 'Everything all right at home?'

'As far as I know.' It sounded silly the moment Peter said it.

'You're not in any trouble, are you?'

'No. Why?'

'Those two questions of mine are ones schoolmasters ask a lot. Or should, even if they do sound trite. You see, Peter, this afternoon's outburst seemed somewhat out of character, and I wondered if there was a reason.'

'No reason. I don't know. I just felt . . . I don't know what I felt.' Peter shook his head and grinned, and then winced. 'I'm sorry I called you a fool.'

The apology was not easy to say, however called for, and Mr Seltman appreciated it.

'Well, we'll put it down to all this hot weather we haven't been having much of. Stress is a funny thing. I wonder – ' Mr Seltman had obviously been about to launch into some excited supposition, but seeing the boredom in Peter's face had checked it. 'Forget it. Off you go.'

'Thanks, Mr Seltman.'

Outside, everyone had gone home except for a solitary figure waiting indistinctly in the bike shed. Patel? No – he was working in the shop this evening. Peter strolled over, swinging his rucksack so that it scraped on the asphalt.

It was Isobel Stanton, who, appearing not to see

him, wheeled out the new bicycle, pausing to fasten the strap on the saddle bag. She bent over to do this, her face averted from Peter, and it was clear to him she had been waiting to catch him 'by chance' and clear, too, the wait had not been too long to carry off the deception with any hope of success.

'Hello.' As she looked up at his greeting the discomfiture in her face supported his theory. 'Lost something?' He gave her the chance to think of a story but she wasn't up to it.

'No, I was just . . . I was . . .'

'You want to leave that pump at home.'

She was grateful he had changed the subject. 'Do I?'

'Yup. Someone'll have it in no time. You've been lucky.'

'Thanks.'

He thought she'd had enough help in this difficult social situation and passed her to wrench his own bike off the rack. She waited for him, composed again. It was his turn to be made to feel awkward.

'How was it?' she asked.

'How was what?'

'Mr What's-his-name. Seltman.'

He shrugged. She wouldn't drop the subject. 'You'd have been for it at my old school.'

'Is that a fact?'

'Yes. It was really strange – you were strange.'

'Thank you – thanks,' he said sourly.

'You don't seem worried about it.'

'That's because I'm not.'

It wasn't true, though he wished it was. He swung his leg over the crossbar of the bike.

'Hang on – don't go.'

This was decision time. He should just say goodbye and belt off. But she was so tenacious she might even chase him, and worse – on that bike – catch him. He remained where he was, sitting on the bike. Stuck. She wheeled her bicycle closer to him.

'Nothing bothers you, does it?'

'I don't know – maybe not.'

'Actually, I waited for you.'

An opening for revenge. He grinned. 'Yes – I know.'

'I wanted to thank you.'

'Oh. Yes . . .' He remembered the Leadbetter incident.

'I thought you were going to hit him.'

'So did he. No, he's not worth it. Anyway, he's all right, really, Barry.'

'He's repulsive.'

'I'll tell him – it'll make his day. Well . . .' He pushed up the pedal, literally about to push off. Mr Seltman drove by them in his Mini, and waved before turning out of the school gates.

'Peter.' Saying his name for the first time was difficult and seemed to invest their conversation with a significance she didn't think it possessed.

'Yes?'

'I was wondering.'

'Yes?'

'You don't have to, but . . . you could come round to our place, maybe, after school one day. Perhaps tomorrow?'

'Oh.' This was exceptionally tricky. He didn't want Barry Leadbetter giving him knowing looks and he knew instinctively that a friendship with Isobel would offend Patel in some way.

'You don't have to.'

She brushed a strand of dark hair from her eyes. They looked at one another. Peter thought of

Professor Stanton. It might be interesting to meet him. He might even ask about the man in Culver Wood. And who cared what people thought anyway. Life was too short. Isobel took his silence to be negative.

'Look – it doesn't matter. No big deal.'

'No – I'll come – great.'

She couldn't keep the gratitude from her eyes. Knew it, hated it. He came to her rescue again.

'Which way do you go?'

'Oh, left out of here, you know . . .'

He had known the answer, but was still relieved. 'I go right. See you tomorrow. OK?'

She let him leave first, watching him work the old bike up to a respectable speed. A friend, perhaps.

# Three

Peter paused at the gate. Had they heard his bicycle? The early evening sun was bright, yet there were trees along the road here, hiding him from the house; he wasn't committed to go any further . . .

The whole thing had got out of hand. The sight of the Professor driving up to the school in the gleaming Range Rover had not had an encouraging effect. The entire school would see him packed into the car, sitting primly with the new girl and her posh, confident father. He could hardly plead that the bicycle wouldn't fit in – the ostentatious vehicle would have taken several. Instead he had muttered that he had to pick up some shopping for his mother and would be along later, and had left the Stantons standing – he imagined – bewildered by their enormous car. The trouble was that his avoidance of the lift had, curiously, left him wishing to avoid the Stantons altogether. This was clearly impossible, his parents knew about the invitation. Last night Peter's mother had been anxious about his clothes, making him feel about as second-rate as it was possible to feel, while his father, whose reaction he had dreaded, had confirmed his worst fears by being tremendously casual about the visit, causing it to assume the status of an audience with Royalty. He had been unable to go home at all and had cycled aimlessly for half an hour before heading very slowly for Isobel's house. And now he felt like heading off again.

'I heard the bike. What are you doing?' Isobel was coming down the path.

'Hi. Um, I think I've got a slow puncture . . .'

'We can always run you home, unless you absolutely have to do something about it now.'

'No, it'll probably be all right.' That would be quite as bad as the lift from school.

'Come on, then.'

He wheeled the bike in through the gate and left it by the fence. They started to walk up the path.

'What do you think of the house?' she asked.

It looked very nice. 'Very nice.'

'Yes, I suppose it is, really. We can take the tea things on to the lawn.'

They did this in silence, as though they were professional caterers and the food was for someone else. The Professor was nowhere to be seen. Nothing is as you imagine it will be. Their conversation was awkward and staccato.

'The cake was Daddy's idea. I don't normally have tea.'

'Nor do I – but it's very nice.'

'You don't have to eat anything if you don't want to.'

'No – it's very nice.'

'Is the tea all right? I made it myself, but it was a long time ago.'

'It's very nice.'

The niceness of everything gagged them for a while. They ate little, neither looking at the other.

Professor Stanton looked up from his desk. Framed between the painted wooden figures, he saw his daughter and her friend sitting quietly on the lawn outside; their slow, careful movements as they ate showed the constraint they were feeling, and Mr Stanton saw no alternative but to go to their rescue. He poured himself a warm gin from the rickety table he called his 'hospitality cabinet', added plenty of tonic water and left the house by the little-used front door.

The boy looked up sharply as Mr Stanton came out of the house and the Professor had a sudden sense of a disturbed character underneath that bland exterior. He might have known Isobel would choose an odd one for a friend . . . But for the moment it was enough that she had come out of her shell sufficiently to make a friend at all.

'How's it going? Any cake left?'

'Tons of it. Help yourself.' Isobel was offhand and her father instinctively pitied her for her imitation of cool dignity. He lay down on his side, resting on an elbow.

'Actually, I don't eat cake. I don't think men do, do they, much?'

Peter swallowed a mouthful of cake and licked his fingers. 'We don't often have it at home. It's very nice.' He thought it sounded as though they couldn't afford cake. 'I don't always like it. Sometimes my mother has to throw it away.' Did that sound any better? He didn't know. The Professor did not appear to have noticed his confusion.

'I wonder how much cake is thrown away every year, to lie festering beneath the earth . . . One of these days I'll go on a dig and end up with my fingers covered in Saxon clotted cream or something.'

Peter's curiosity stirred. 'I suppose you do find interesting things, don't you? When you go on a dig.'

'Toast, marmalade, fried eggs – the lot.'

'Don't be silly, Daddy,' Isobel said.

'Why not? Are you interested, ah, Peter? Not many people are.'

'Well, I'm interested in history. Reading about it.'

'Perhaps you'll come along one day, when I get things humming around here.'

'No. I don't think so,' Peter said abruptly.

'Your decision. You can if you like, anyway.'

'You're going to dig in Culver Wood, aren't you?' The boy sounded almost angry.

'I'll probably start there.'

'Why?'

'Got to start somewhere . . .' Mr Stanton was vague.

'I was there the other day. There was a man there.'

'Oh yes?'

'I thought he might be something to do with you.'

'Not that I'm aware of. I've only seen the place in passing myself.'

'So why do you want to dig it up?'

Isobel came in. 'They're very careful – after all, the last thing Daddy wants to do is to damage anything.'

Peter persisted. 'I still don't understand why Culver Wood.' The Professor looked at him for a moment. For some reason the boy really wanted to know.

'Well, it's a long story, but . . . Well, OK.' He considered his approach. 'What do you know about Culver Wood?'

'Nothing at all. It's just a wood.'

'OK. You've never heard any old tales about "don't go down there, young man" or legends about its being haunted?'

'No. It's not.'

'I don't suppose for a moment it is. But going

through archive material one finds reference to it as, well, somewhere with a bad reputation – somewhere local folk were leery of, a long, long time ago. Which is where I come in. Two years ago I discovered a small temple to the Roman God Mithras. This was near York, at a place surrounded by ancient legends of witchcraft. You see, the Mithras cult was superceded by Christianity and the early Christians were strongly against Mithras, precisely because his religion was in some ways akin to theirs and so represented a real threat to their beliefs. There was fear, therefore, and where there's fear there's violence and superstition and old wives' tales. If I hadn't this slight, but very similar, evidence here – this *feel* for Culver Wood – I wouldn't bother with this part of England at all. Archaeologically, it's been worked to death – every mile of ground has been turned over like some great kitchen garden. But Mithras is my obsession, so . . . here I am.' He smiled at Isobel. 'Here *we* are.'

'Do you go on these archaeological diggings?' Peter asked Isobel.

'I used to, a bit. It's not very interesting. You'd be surprised how boring it is.' She sounded quite venomous. Peter glanced at the Professor, looking for a clue as to how he should take this. Mr Stanton did not react at all. It was as if he had not heard the dismissive remarks – or was used to them.

'When are you starting?' Peter's question did not stir the Professor. 'Mr Stanton? Professor?'

Isobel's father sipped his drink, then looked at Peter, smiling.

'. . . It's Jim.' Peter was not expecting this, and nor was Isobel, as he noticed. She looked blank. Jim . . . *I'll do you the courtesy of treating you as an adult.* His father's phrase, used in argument, came to Peter. He felt uncomfortable.

'Oh right . . . When are you starting in Culver Wood?'

The Professor seemed quite at ease. 'Oh, you know – whenever. There's no hurry. I'm getting a team together. It all takes time . . . You two be all right, will you? I'd better get back to . . . things . . .' He got to his feet and strolled back to the house.

Isobel looked pleased with herself. 'Something I said?'

'What do you mean?'

'And you've got to call him Jim . . .!' The implicit ill-feeling between father and daughter embarrassed Peter.

'Well, why not?'

'Oh, I don't know. He seems to like you, anyway. He doesn't talk to me like that – like he did to you. That was all news to me.' Peter suspected that if the Professor – *Jim* – was not forthcoming to Isobel, it was because she discouraged his confidences.

'Yes – it was interesting, wasn't it?'

The Professor poured himself another drink. There appeared now to be more animation on the lawn, so his mission had not been in vain. The warm gin tasted like some kind of household cleaning fluid – he had forgotten to put in more tonic. Isobel was determined to be a problem. If he spent time with her she ignored him, and when he wanted to work she was somehow always there, forcing herself to the centre of his attention, helpless and hurt and apparently disliking him intensely.

'He's such a show-off.'

'Your father? I didn't think so. You should see mine – and he's got nothing to show off *about*.' That was a betrayal. 'No, he's great, really, but . . . you know.' He felt better after this vague retraction. 'I still don't really get it, though. Why you're here.'

'My mother died. Daddy wanted a change of scene. I think he's going to get himself attached to a university here, eventually. He's a great fixer. We've got a video.'

This seemed an abrupt change of tack. 'Oh, yes?'

'He gets it off tax because he lectures. And they get him on TV sometimes.'

'We haven't got a video.'

'They're great.'

'Yeah – I know.'

'Well, if there's anything you want to see . . .'

Isobel appeared to be quite a fixer herself, and obviously prepared to bribe her way into favour with Peter. It was flattering in a way; but why had she picked on him. . . ?

It was almost fully dark when Peter started his journey home. It had been surprising how well he and Isobel had got on. You wouldn't have thought they had anything in common, on the face of it. But then of course Isobel had no friends here yet, and if she'd singled him out it was probably only because he was approachable; easy going. He realized, thinking about it, that it wasn't as if her friendship could much disturb the pattern of his life. When you thought about it, he himself didn't have many real friends here. There was Patel – who was another 'outsider' – and . . . who else? That was funny. Why hadn't it occurred to him before? Everyone was very friendly and he was friendly enough himself, but no one other than Patel qualified as a friend, really. How funny, that he hadn't thought of that before. Not that it mattered.

Culver Wood. He was nearing Culver Wood. His bicycle had apparently come this way of its own volition. The Professor's hopes of the place leapt into his mind. *Witchcraft. Violence and superstition. The Roman God Mithras. A temple.* What nonsense. Peter quickened the bike's pace. Culver Wood was a place he'd known all his life. A place that was peaceful – welcoming, even. He'd spend some time there now; although he wouldn't be able to see anything, it would prove how safe the wood was, how silly these long-forgotten old wives' tales were. He arrived at the edge of the wood and lowered the bike to the ground as he dismounted, in one easy movement. He went to the outermost of the old beech trees and stopped dead. The back of his neck prickled and he turned round quickly to the road. Nothing, nothing there. He turned again to the wood and it felt as though water was moving just under the skin on his back, running outwards from his spine. He couldn't bring himself to enter the wood. The silence was complete; nothing moved, not Peter, not a single leaf.

It was the man he had seen there that had caused this change in Peter's attitude. That must be it. If he went on into the wood, might he not come across the man again, his deep-sunken eyes invisible in the gloom, watching without a word? *Who was he?* If not the Professor's man, then whose? Peter was now convinced the man had been there with a purpose. He forced himself to shift from where he stood, forced himself to move to his bike at what he guessed was a normal pace. Picking up the bicycle, he mounted and rode away, pressing his feet down hard on the pedals, but with control, as if out for routine exercise and for the fresh air which cooled his forehead, while all the time fear stuck in his chest like an arrowhead.

'No, really, Peter, I was worried. It's not right. They must have a telephone – all it would have taken was a quick call.' His mother was wide-eyed with reproach. 'I'm not after you all the time like some mothers – you live your own life and welcome. I'm not a nosey-parker – but you've got to tell me where you are and what's going on. *I* don't know their address or phone number – you knew that – or I'd have phoned myself. It's not fair.' She seemed childishly bewildered at what a shocking world it was. Peter had no patience with her.

'What's the problem? I'd have been home by eight-thirty but I went for a ride – it's nothing to get stupid about.'

'Wait till you're a parent.'

'I will.'

Mrs Ford wore an apron over a patterned dress that had seen better days. She presented a very solitary figure as she went back to the washing-up which his return had interrupted.

'Well, there's no food for you. Nor your Dad. I threw it away.'

'I don't want any. Where's Dad?'

'He'll have to make do with bread-and-something. There's no cheese.'

'Where is he?'

'Down the pub. At least I know where *he* is . . .'

Peter at once had a vision of his father at the bar in the Swan Inn. *'Young Peter's made a friend. Her father's on the television sometimes. He's a bright lad, Peter.'* Peter went out of the kitchen and up the narrow stairs. His mother left the tap running and came after him to the foot of the stairs, typically abandoning her grievances.

'Anything wrong? Don't you want to watch some telly'

He stopped at the top of the stairs. 'No. I'm going to bed, I think. I'm tired.'

'You're not ill, are you? What did you have for tea?'

'What?'

'I didn't ask you how the tea went. Come and tell me about it.'

'No. It was all right.'

'You had a good time?'

'Yeah – it was all right.'

'That's good, anyway. 'Night-night if I don't see you.'

'Yeah, 'night Mum.'

The central light bulb had 'gone' in Peter's room. His mother had shut the curtains and Peter took pleasure in his instinctive knowledge, acquired over the years, of just where everything was in the room. He undressed in the dark, putting on a T-shirt and shorts in lieu of pyjamas before finding the switch to the bedside light. The little room sprang into unwelcoming life.

Unlike others of his age, he treated his bedroom simply as a place to rest. He had never bothered to clutter it with possessions and things to hang on the walls, with the effect that the bare room at least looked larger than it was. He went along the landing to brush his teeth in the bathroom. Downstairs his mother had turned on the television for the ten o'clock news. Going back to his room, Peter now rather regretted he hadn't apologized for being so late. He had not realized just how far he had cycled after leaving Culver Wood.

He sat on the bed. Professor Stanton wanted a 'find'. That had been Isobel's cynical view of her father. Apparently he was a man in some ways similar to Mr Ford, one who, in his own words, always 'had an eye to the main chance'. So Culver Wood was interesting to the Professor only because it seemed a likely place to look . . .

It came to Peter that he had been waiting for this last thought to arrive. It was important. Now he was tired. He got into bed and turned off the light.

It was still dark when Mrs Ford came down the stairs the next morning, drawn to the sounds of movement in the kitchen.

'Peter? What are you doing?'

'Sorry, Mum. Did I wake you up?'

'Yes. What are you doing?' She kept her voice low, though it was unlikely any amount of noise would wake her husband, who was lying upstairs like a stunned rhinoceros, having last night fallen into the convivial company of Mr Williams from next door.

'I'm leaving early for school,' Peter said, folding an unbuttered slice of bread and taking a bite from the middle.

'Oh. I thought you'd forgotten some homework.'

'Didn't have any.'

Mrs Ford looked out of the window, where the darkness was being washed into a silver grey. 'It's raining again.'

'Not much. It'll get better.'

'The school'll be shut.'

'Yes, well, I'm just going to have a ride around.'

She smiled a tired smile. 'Feeling frisky?'

It sounded animal rather than human but Peter agreed for the sake of brevity. 'Yes.'

'Don't catch cold. Well, now I'm down here . . .' Mrs Ford began to take last night's washing-up from the draining board and put it away, and Peter went out into the light, sleeting rain. As he opened the gate, pushing his bike in front of him, he heard his mother's alarm clock go off. He waited. Ten to one she hadn't gone back upstairs. There – his father's voice, raised in complaint. Serve him right. Feeling strangely uplifted, Peter cycled off, away from the route to school, in the direction of Aldington.

It was only half an hour later, when, uncomfortably wet, a less ebullient Peter began to wonder what he was doing. He had circled Aldington Frith, had raced down Clap Hill before turning left towards Sellindge and was now coming back only a few miles from where he had started. As he went, he looked over into fields, into woods, even into private gardens, being thoroughly nosey, as though he was looking for something. It was fun in a way, yet tiring, like shopping for a present with no idea of what to get or even what sort of shop to try. After a while his travels took on the aspect of a time-killing exercise, purposeless and dull. The rain had somehow entered his brain, leaving it sodden and incapable of any thought except 'Pointless. This is pointless,'

He was not consciously aware when the rain ceased to fall. He found he was passing Culver Wood, finally heading for school. His legs felt heavy and when he saw the man standing in the shelter of the great trees he was unable to drive the bike faster. The man wore the same clothes as before. Their eyes met as Peter passed him and, as if by a mutual understanding, neither allowed the faintest glimmer of recognition to reach their faces. It was only as he reached the school gates that Peter felt a sting of regret that he had not stopped and asked the man just why it was he hung around Culver Wood like that. Then his mind drifted again.

He went into the school paying little attention to his surroundings. There was a human traffic jam outside the classroom and Peter waited stolidly as it resolved itself. Isobel arrived at his side.

'Hello, Peter.' She felt shy and was sure it showed. Peter turned to her.

'Hi.' He looked utterly calm, yet to Isobel it seemed that he focused his eyes through hers to the back of her head, his gaze intense but almost unseeing.

'Thanks for coming yesterday.' He did not answer, only smiled in a non-committal fashion, making Isobel feel excluded and unsure of herself. Perhaps he didn't want to know her after all. Perhaps she had bored him yesterday. She smiled back at him, deliberately keeping her eyes dead. He didn't seem to notice the intended snub and they went into the classroom and began another school day.

Isobel was determined that it would not be she who made the next friendly move and pointedly ignored Peter throughout the first morning period. It was not a successful strategy; he didn't notice. He seemed to be concentrating fully on the lesson, frowning and following every word spoken in the course of the class as though he were keen to catch up on school work after a long illness. To Isobel it all seemed aimed cruelly at her, he didn't want to know her and wanted to demonstrate this.

It was not until the first break that she began to take a less personal view of Peter's behaviour. The second lesson over, the class trailed out to the wet asphalt of the recreation areas. At the door, Isobel looked back at Peter. He sat at his desk idly running a hand over the wood of the desk-top, his head down. Patel came up to him from the back of the room.

'Hey, Dopey.'

'Hi, Patel.' Peter spoke quietly and Isobel had to listen hard to follow his side of the conversation.

'What have you got on tonight?' Patel waited for repartee from this opening and had eventually to supply it himself. 'Football boots and a wet T-shirt?' Since Peter only had the grace to smile at this, Patel laughed for him. 'No, seriously, what are you doing?'

'I don't know. I'm tired.'

'It's great now for nesting – eggs, you know.' Patel had a passion for climbing trees and Peter sometimes went along with him.

'No. I really am tired. Not today.'

'What have you been up to, eh?'

'Nothing.' Peter continued to run his fingers along the desk and Patel gave him up as a lost cause.

'Suit yourself.'

Isobel still waited at the door as Patel went out, and he gave her a distinctly unfriendly look, almost pushing past her through the doorway. She walked back over to Peter.

'Anything wrong?' He looked up at this and smiled. She was relieved to see his smile was genuine and then wondered why she cared.

'No, nothing's wrong?' His smile faded. 'That's what Seltman asked me the other day, doing his family welfare bit.'

'I'm glad you came over yesterday.'

'Me too.'

'Are you just going to sit there or are you coming outside?'

'I'll stay here for a bit. See you.' It was a form of dismissal and Isobel found she had no choice but to accept it.

Later she saw him leaning against one of the prefabs, alone. She did not go over. He still liked her; that was what she had wanted to know, and she would respect his privacy.

The morning had been spring; the afternoon made the indefinable leap to early summer. After the rain, the air was hot and moist, steaming out tensions from the classroom to such a degree that it was impossible to get worked up about anything much, let alone a Maths lesson.

Peter was exhausted now, yet a question had wound itself into a knot in his brain. *What did I think I was doing this morning?* He wished the day would end. School did. He packed his rucksack very slowly, unaware Isobel was looking at him, standing right at his side. She thought of saying something, then put her hand on his arm. He did not react. Well, no matter. She left with the others, to whom energy was returning. To Peter the rising noise level was no more than a distant sound, so commonplace as hardly to register at all.

By the time he left the bike shed, all but the most compulsive stragglers had left the school. He wheeled out the old bike and set off at a snail's pace towards Culver Wood. It was ridiculous to be wary of a place he so liked; and there was, he told himself, only the very remotest chance the man would be there again.

Peter wanted there to be nothing alarming about the wood. And he realized too that he wanted it left alone by all other people. Like the Professor, as well as the stranger. He tried to convince himself the man in the tweed hat must seem familiar because he looked like an actor, or someone on television. Surely that must be the reason . . .

He felt less tired by the time he arrived at the side of the trees. As he had cycled along, every metre closer to the wood had brought fresh life to him. He dropped the bike, vaulted the fencing and strode into the tall trees. Immediately he was confident. Nothing had changed. It was his place, unaltered by the stranger's presence or by the Professor's hopes that there had been untoward happenings her in the past. He went to the clearing he liked and sat for a while on the serpentine tree root. it was friendly here; even the ever-changing patterns of light seemed to be going through a cycle he had seen before. Peter felt alert again for the first time since leaving the house that morning. *It's all right,* he thought. He walked on to the point where the trees thinned and the far-off Channel glinted through them like beaten steel. Standing here in the old wood, the roads and fields and the scattered houses below him seemed new and impermanent.

About two hundred metres to his right, well beyond the wood, the large garden of a private house extended to the edge of the land-bound cliff. Peter was envious of the owners of the house; they had it made, living exactly where he would like to live. He wondered what the wood looked like from over there. He had never quite dared to do any trespassing before, but today, now, it seemed the thing to do.

The house itself was an ugly, angular, white building with many large square windows, evidently designed more to look out of than to be looked at. Peter felt uneasy and exposed under its gaze, stranded on the open spaces of the sloping lawn. The wood had not looked interesting from where he now stood: if anything it would irritate the owners of the house, as it partially blocked their panoramic view of the Romney Marsh and the town of Hythe.

Even further from Culver Wood, on the other side of the fastidiously kept garden, the land was intriguingly uncared for. Hummocks of grass-tufted earth rolled away for some distance. A weatherbeaten sign stood at an angle there, as if peering over the cliff, and Peter found himself curious to see what it read. He climbed the peeling garden fence and felt the comfortable, springy turf under his feet. Nearer to, he saw the sign showed the letters M.O.D. and warned that this too was not public ground. The Ministry of Defence owned a great deal of land around the Kent coast and Peter was unsurprised. He saw that by lying down between two of the grassy mounds he would not be visible from the big white house and, feeling a resurgence of his tiredness, sank down there.

The M.O.D. had apparently enlisted armies of rabbits to guard their property, for there were droppings and burrows everywhere. The ground was warm but after a while yielded up a damp reminder of the morning rain, and Peter rolled over on to his knees. His hand stretched out to the closest rabbit burrow and he scrabbled at the loose earth with his fingers, imagining that deep in the warren a rabbit might recognize these movements as friendly and come up for a look. More likely the creature would think just the reverse and go deeper. He let the soil fall through his fingers. Something else fell to the grass. He picked it up from the scattered earth he had let fall: an unevenly-rounded disc. An army dog tag? Perhaps not; it was too heavy somehow. He picked at the impacted earth that covered it, revealing an old coin of some sort, more perfectly rounded than it had at first seemed. Perhaps there were more of these here, perhaps even one of those treasure troves . . . He again dug his fingers into the burrow and then withdrew them sharply. That was no coin. He pared away the earth more carefully and used his fingers as tweezers to draw the object out. Even to Peter's untrained eye its use was apparent. It was a triangular, tapering spearhead that had long outlasted its wooden shaft.

It was only now as he sat there exhilarated, clutching these fragments from the past, that he realized there had been a purpose to his bike ride that morning. It had been to find the Professor an alternative site for his dig. All that looking into fields, peering into people's gardens . . . Foolishly – subconsciously – he had been looking for just what he now had, something to distract Mr Stanton from Culver Wood. What a piece of luck! He began to scratch at the coin with his nails. Just wait till the Professor saw this.

A sick feeling of disgust stopped Peter from trying to uncover the coin's secret. He was no archaeologist. Leave it to Isobel's father to dirty his hands. Yes – 'dirty his hands'. How horrible, to deal in the past, to root about amongst dead people's possessions. Peter's feeling of revulsion was so strong that he dropped the coin as if it were infectious.

To hand these things over to the Professor would be to betray someone, somehow. He wouldn't do it. And yet . . .

# Four

'You don't understand, Bella. The boy doesn't want any credit. He doesn't want anything to do with it.'

The two statues, heads inclined, seemed especially motionless this evening.

'Doesn't that depend on what you said – how you talked to him?'

'If you'd been here, you'd have seen. He was definite about it. There was nothing I could say to make him change his mind.'

'How hard did you try?'

'Hard, I can promise you. I didn't deceive him and I'm not trying to deceive you now!' Professor Stanton's voice was raised. Isobel continued in her role as cool prosecuting counsel.

'Did you tell him he could be on TV?'

'Judging from his attitude, that would be the last thing he wants.'

'Did you tell him he could get some money for finding these things?'

'No, because he won't – he can't. It's government land. He shouldn't have been there in the first place.'

Isobel appeared to come to a decision. 'All right.' She went to the door and turned. 'You should have told me he was here.'

'He came to see *me*, Bella. I didn't know where you were.'

'I was only in the orchard.'

'I didn't know that. I don't spy on your every movement.'

'It doesn't matter,' said Isobel in a tone that succeeded only in concealing the exact degree of neglect she felt. She lingered at the door and the Professor guessed the reason.

'Have another look. It's fascinating, isn't it?' He turned to the trestle tables and picked up the spearhead. 'When you think that – ' She had gone, leaving the door open. Mr Stanton went to the door and looked up the dim staircase. She must be moving quietly, as she had when she was little and wanted to see who had come to dinner or drinks. His daughter's practised stealth was disconcerting. He looked at the spearhead in his hand and suddenly felt a draught from the window. Closing the door, he went back to the line of trestle tables.

The coin reposed in a once-clear fluid in a small glass tray. The solution was muddied now as the cleansing agents worked. Any minute now the Professor would examine the coin and . . . The familiar feeling of pleasurable anxiety came over him. Coins tended to be 'self-dating'. It really was the most incredible good fortune.

The spearhead had a distinct ridge running through it, a rib effect that had suggested he was dealing with a weapon of war of the first few centuries after the birth of Christ. Its size was greater than that of the Roman fighting spear. The strongest possibility was that it was Gallic or Germanic in origin, and either the property of an early invader after the departure of the Roman legions or that of a late foreign conscript to the Roman cause. While certain archaeologists would be hopeful they were in the later period, in order to add to theories about an early fifth century German invasion of the south of England, Mr Stanton's interest would be greater if the artifacts were of the period of Roman occupation.

He must sound out the Ministry of Defence before the weekend. There shouldn't be a problem, apart from the initial one of explaining why it was he wanted to explore their ground. His approach could be to express interest in the site simply because of its proximity to the nearest archaeological excavation, of whatever kind, that he found in the records. A 'white lie'. The Professor thought about Peter again. He had been so very adamant he did not want to be involved in any way. And then dashing off like that, apparently uncurious as to the exact nature of his find . . . Very odd.

Peter stared at the television in the darkened front room. He had not turned on any of the lights and the room was lit solely by the glare of the song and dance act in front of him. He would go to bed soon. In the meantime it was relaxing to think of nothing and use the television as an instrument of hypnotism rather than entertainment.

In the kitchen Mrs Ford sliced onions in a basin of water. She had heard on the radio that this stopped you crying and so far it was working. The music from the television was lively and though she was not sure of the tune, she hummed along all the same.

Professor Stanton removed the coin from the tray and dried it thoroughly. Throughout the whole process he had refused to look at it; like a schoolboy he wanted to see it only when it was in a condition to give up its secret. That it was gold had been certain from the moment he had set eyes and hands on it. Weighty, uncorroded . . . He gave the coin a last rub and opened up the damp cloth. Yes. Gold. A deep, old gold. Gold, the metal used in the mints of the late Roman Empire of the West. An iron die had stamped on to the soft metal a superbly crafted portrait. Theodosius, briefly Theodosius the Great, Emperor of both the Western and Eastern Empires near the very end of the fourth century AD. His successor to the Western Empire, Constantine the Third, was believed to have presided over the withdrawal from Britain of the last Roman troops. Exultation welled up in the Professor's throat. This could be fascinating indeed. Let there be more. Let there be more. He was the right man in the right place at the right time. Let there be more . . .

Peter was in high spirits as he hurtled through the school gate, scattering four pedestrians from a lower form. The sun was already beating down strongly and he was truly carefree. Free of care, thinking not of the past or of the future but only of how tremendously pleasant it was to be Peter Ford on a morning in May, he swept majestically to the bike shed.

In the shed Barry Leadbetter was conducting a transaction with Jack Bennett.

'All right. All three for four pounds. I've hardly played them.'

Jack hesitated, holding the cassette recordings loosely, as though a firmer grip on them would commit him to a purchase. Leadbetter pressed his advantage.

'Oh come on. You know you want them. They're immaculate – look at them – not a scratch.'

Jack looked miserably undecided. 'That's just the cases. You can't tell what they're like inside.'

'Don't bother, then, I've got better things to do than hang about here.'

That clinched it. 'No – no. I'll have them.'

'Give us the money, then.' Reluctantly, Bennett parted with the four coins. He walked off with his head down, as if depressed by his acquisition. Leadbetter winked at Peter.

'All right, Pete?'

'Yeah, not bad, Barry.'

'You look pleased with yourself. You like having a girlfriend, do you?'

Peter had expected this kind of comment. It didn't bother him. 'What amazes me about you, Barry, is that no one's ever re-arranged your features for you. They'd be doing you a favour, you know.' They walked together towards the school.

'I hope you're not too tired to play this afternoon.' Barry was still smirking.

'What?'

'Football.'

'Oh yes . . . That's right.' Peter remembered. He would have to borrow football gear for the practice match. He had forgotten all about it.

When they entered the classroom, Isobel smiled warmly at him. Peter wished she hadn't. Leadbetter nudged him so hard he lost his balance.

'Pack it in!'

Leadbetter smiled broadly and sauntered to the back of the classroom. Though the clock showed there was a minute or so to go before class started, Mr Jarvis, Geography, was already at the blackboard, carefully scalloping the outline of a map of Norway, referring to an atlas propped open at the bottom of the board. Isobel kept her voice low.

'Why didn't you come and find me last night?'

'Didn't seem any point. I had to get back.'

'Daddy wants to see you again.'

For some reason this made Peter inwardly restless. 'Why?'

'Tell you later.'

Mr Jarvis turned from his work of art.

'Norway. Abundant hydroelectric resources.'

'Why?'

A group of girls came down the corridor past Peter and Isobel, giggling and whispering their assumption that the two were discussing an assignation.

'Because – well, obviously because he wants to talk to you.' Isobel was patient with Peter, who looked at the retreating girls with annoyance.

'I don't see why, though.'

'You can't just walk in with those things and expect him to say thanks very much and leave it at that.'

Stated so clearly, Peter saw it was exactly what he had wanted Mr Stanton to do. He frowned. 'When?'

Isobel had not been given any instructions on this, but was prepared to act on her own authority for her own purposes.

'Saturday. Come to lunch. Don't say you can't, because I won't believe you.'

'Yeah. All right,' Peter said ungraciously. 'Look I've got to borrow some football gear. See you.'

After lunch Peter and the other footballers disappeared. He had patently avoided further talk with Isobel, and she imagined she knew the cause of this; he was embarrassed by the idea his friends might mentally pair them off. It was understandable that he wanted to stifle such speculation.

To his disgust Peter found he was playing on the 'B'

team today, which indicated he was unlikely to be picked for the Under-Sixteens side for the forthcoming challenge match with another local school. He had not been aware his form had been poor of late and was conscious that, on the 'B' team, a speedy left winger such as himself would not often receive the ball with a chance to go forward with it, as he would have to spend most of the afternoon defending.

The sportsmaster encouraged both sides with shrieked abuse. His powerful voice was deadened by the heavy atmosphere. Grey, discoloured clouds obscured the sun and cast a metallic light on the scene. Peter went into a sliding tackle and chased the resulting loose ball, stopping it on the touchline only to be swept, ball and all, into touch by the 'A' team player he had dispossessed. It was that sort of game. His left thigh felt bruised and he got up slowly.

'All right, lad?'

He nodded to the sportsmaster, and placed a long throw all the way back to the goalkeeper, who shouted 'Get forward – go on!' before slicing the ball to a cluster of players hovering at the edge of the penalty area. Peter watched the ensuing fracas without enthusiasm.

A spitting drone of engines made him look up. Out of the low clouds appeared an old-fashioned propeller plane, flying steadily above the football field. Its compact, predatory shape was familiar to Peter from films of the Second World War. It was a Spitfire or a Hurricane. He could just see the colours of the roundels – the recognition circles on the plane's body. No one else was looking at the plane; a goal was about to be scored. Shouts drew Peter's attention and he watched as the ball bounced off the diving goal-keeper's legs, was headed back against the bar and fell again to the feet of one of the 'A' team. He hesitated and then played the ball to his captain, who was prevented from further action when the whistle went.

'Half-time!' the sportsmaster announced busily. 'That'll teach you not to muck about like that. All right, change ends now. Chop-chop.'

The two teams began to straggle past each other to the opposite halves of the pitch, and Patel wandered up gloomily to Peter. 'We were lucky there. Where were you, then?'

Peter stared after the aeroplane, which was about to sink behind distant trees. 'It was a Hurricane.' Yes – that's what it was. The hump-backed fuselage was unmistakable, and the shape of the wings viewed from below and – how did he suddenly know all this? His mind raced. He had seen such planes before. In a dream? No, in reality. An air show? But he had never been to one . . . A submerged memory started to float up to the surface, to be sunk again by the sound of Patel's voice.

'A Hurricane? What was?' He was mystified. The aeropane dipped from view. 'What are you talking about?'

It was then that it occurred to Peter that no one else had commented on the unusual sight. It dawned on him that of the almost two dozen people on the pitch, *only he had seen the plane*. He felt sweat break out on his cold forehead.

'You don't half look odd.' Patel was still by his side. 'Come on.'

When they had taken up their positions the whistle sounded and the game went on as before, with the 'A' team flattening Leadbetter and gaining possession of the ball within seconds.

Patel looked over at Peter once more. 'Are you ill?'

'No. Let's get on with it.'

Peter played the rest of the game as if his life depended on it. It was a conscious decision to involve himself fully in a process that did not allow him time to think.

Seconds before the final whistle went, he was actually able to dodge his way through the 'A' team defence to set up Patel with a perfect scoring chance, only for his friend to lift his head and blast the ball wide of the goal. Though his side had been well-beaten, Peter discovered that he had at least won the approval of the sportsmaster, who held him up to the others of the 'B' team as a model of application and enthusiasm. Peter was unmoved by the praise, which further impressed the master.

'You'll have to wait until I post the team on the board like everyone else, but I can tell you you've every reason to feel satisfied with your work this afternoon.' Peter smiled as he was meant to. 'It's attitude that counts with me,' the sportsmaster went on. 'Not that you haven't got a bit of skill, too,' he said as he moved on. But the once-coveted praise meant little now: something inexplicable was happening in Peter's life and he was frightened.

In the neon-lit changing room, the hiss of the showers and the accompanying steam did nothing to calm Peter as he washed the borrowed football gear in a basin. Patel, bright-eyed, glistening, his wet hair apparently sellotaped to his head, adjusted the knot of his school tie.

'Going home dirty?'

'I don't know.'

'Fancy going into Folkestone?'

'Nah.'

'You're getting to be a bore.'

'Sure.'

'I mean it, Pete.'

'OK, you mean it.'

'You're a bore.'

'I heard you the first time.'

'What's up with you?' The showers hissed on, though the last of the footballers was leaving now. 'I don't want to spend time with a bore.'

Peter looked up, uninvolved. 'Don't, then.' The reply to this might well have been 'I won't, then,' but Patel was determined to get a positive response from Peter.

'Just because you're good at football, it doesn't make you a superstar, you know.'

'That's right.'

A pause. 'Nine times out of ten I would have scored that goal.'

'That's the way it goes . . .'

Patel had only succeeded in making himself angry. 'I don't get it. What's wrong with you?' Peter started to wring out the clothing. 'Anyway, I don't care.'

Patel left quickly and Peter was conscious their relationship was irrevocably altered. The tolerant Indian had been a close friend these past years, but one cannot keep friends close if one excludes them from confidences. 'I'm going mad, Pat – I saw an old aeroplane but there wasn't one.' He tried the words out loud.

'Turn it all off, will you, when you go?' The captain of the Under-Sixteens and the 'A team, whose temporary responsibility the changing rooms were, had popped his head around the door in brief acknowledgement of his duties. 'You the last? Turn it all off then. You had a good game.'

'Thanks.' The captain's head withdrew. Suppose this last exchange had not taken place; had been imaginary? Peter almost felt like going to the door to call the football captain back, to reassure himself. But it would be too silly. They both existed, in solid normality. The aeroplane had seemed tangible and ordinary, too . . .

*Ordinary*. That was the crucial word. At some time Peter had seen hundreds of such aeroplanes – they had been as familiar to him as the passenger planes of today. In another life? A 'previous life'? There were those who believed in reincarnation – who claimed they had lived before. Mostly they met with a sceptical reaction though, and he personally knew no one who would take him seriously if he were to talk about his experience. So – he wouldn't tell anyone. There wasn't a choice, really. It was something of a relief to reach this point in his thoughts. He decided to take a shower after all. Yes . . . If one could not understand such a strange occurrence, perhaps the only solution was just to ignore it.

As the water cascaded down on to him, he relaxed still more. There was nothing he could do. He felt alert, healthy as anyone could feel, and could now allow the possibility – remote as it was – that there *had* been an aeroplane, a relic from some museum or something, and by some strange coincidence nobody else had seen it. The weirdest coincidences did happen. It was common knowledge. He actually started to whistle, happy in his own company.

On Saturday morning Peter had no inclination to whistle.

'Wait a second, I'll just get a coffee. Do you want anything?' Peter, already sitting, stuck, in the study, shook his head and Mr Stanton smiled and left the room.

It seemed somehow *official* to be talking here in the first place, and now he was to wait alone as though for his headmaster before an admonition of some sort. He sat rigidly upright in the chair, with no conception of how to make himself feel at ease or even how to fake it. He had no desire to wander about looking at the Professor's belongings or work, so he sweated it out miserably until the owner of the room returned.

Coffee mug in hand, the archaeologist looked comfortable as he slipped into his own leather chair behind his own desk in his own room. Peter was unreasonably resentful of this.

When Isobel came in, following her father from the kitchen, where she had been helping Mrs Davies make a salad for lunch, he felt no lessening of tension: now he was outnumbered. Isobel saw with surprise how defensive he had become as he sat with his arms tightly folded. He had seemed his usual placid self when she had greeted him at the door. Her father smiled.

'Well, young man.' If anything, Isobel flinched more than Peter at this form of address. 'We have some unfinished business, do we not?'

'I don't think so. Do we?'

'Your coin was very interesting. Here. Look.'

Peter reluctantly took the proffered coin. 'Very nice.'

'I don't think you realize what it is you stumbled on. That's about fifteen hundred years old.'

Peter attempted a joke. 'Won't buy much now then. Inflation and all that . . .'

'That's one way of looking at it!' The Professor was unrelentingly friendly. 'What have you been doing since I last saw you?'

'Oh . . . school . . . you know. Not a lot.'

'I've been busy. It looks like I've got permission to excavate this site.'

'Have you?'

'Yes. I thought . . . well, I thought since you started this, you might like to help – after school, the weekends, holidays. Now you've had time to think about it. It's exciting, being part of a dig.'

Isobel chipped in. 'It's a great honour.' Her tone held the faintest suggestion of mockery.

'Anyway, I'd like you to be involved. I'd like it very much. You wouldn't be out of place or anything. We always have what you might call amateur participation. We couldn't manage without it.'

Peter would not be moved. 'I'm sorry. I'm still not interested.'

'All right. I'm not going to get pushy about it. But I don't understand – I really don't . . . Unless there's something about the site you haven't told me.'

The weighty silence that now fell showed Peter that this was the key question. 'I don't know what you mean.'

'Well, look at if from my angle. It's possible you've pointed me to the site of a settlement or a burial ground. That's what I'm hoping for, anyway. But on the other hand . . .' The Professor was uncertain of how to continue. '. . . what you've given me could be the sum total of the find, now and hereafter – After a great deal of time and work we might not come up with anything more. And when you come down to it, I've only got your word for it that you found what you've brought me where you said you found it.'

Peter was speechless with indignation, but Isobel jumped in. 'That's not fair, Daddy! That's a terrible thing to say! It's like you think Peter's trying to trick you!'

'I doubt it, Isobel – but how can I tell? He's not the least bit enthusiastic about this – he wants no part of it from the outset. It's only human to have doubts. Then, perhaps he doesn't want to help because he knows damn well it would be a waste of time. That's a suspicious but very natural reaction to have. Do you both see that?'

This acceptance of a natural alliance between Peter and Isobel was a source of strength to Peter. 'Look, I was doing you a favour. At least I thought I was. I told you the truth – honestly. Anyone could have found those things. It happened to be me, and I knew about you, and . . . I thought you'd be pleased – not . . .'

If Peter was prepared to control his temper, Isobel, on home ground, was not. 'I think you're foul, Daddy!'

Even in his anger the middle class phrase jarred, alienating Peter from Isobel. Really, it was him against the Stantons, as he had feared.

'I don't mean to be foul, Bella.' The Professor left it at that.

'Well, I'm sorry,' said Peter, 'I can't help what you think. I've told you the truth and that's it.'

Mr Stanton looked at him, felt sorry for him, believed him. 'All right, Peter.' He couldn't help himself, 'But you do see what I mean? It's so very odd – I meet you one day and the next you're putting me on to something that some archaeologists wait all their lives for. If, that is—' He had the sense to stop there. 'Just tell me again how you came across the artifacts – what you gave me.'

Peter said wearily, 'I was bored; I was just killing time, you know? And I thought I'd take a look at a place I'd never been. I didn't think too much about trespassing or anything. I was just passing the time. I lay down and – it was quite nice there – and, I don't know, I was just sort of mucking about. There were these rabbit holes and . . . that's it . . .'

'These things arrived in your hand, by coincidence?'

'No – they . . . Well, sort of, yes.'

'Just one of those things. Just a coincidence.'

'Yes, if you like. Just one of those things.'

'A coincidence.'

Peter found he was shaking. He got up. His voice was pitched high. 'Why do you keep saying that?'

'Saying what?' The boy's sudden distress bewildered the Professor.

'Coincidence. What's wrong with that? Coincidences do happen, don't they?'

'I suppose so.' How did one react to this?

'Well, they do! All the time – they happen all the time!'

'Yes, I suppose they must.'

'Of course they do! Everyone knows that – you read about it – all the time!' Peter was pleading now. 'Just believe me!'

Both the Stantons were upset. Peter's emotion was embarrassing, naked. Isobel could not look at him. Her father did, pretending for Peter's sake that this was quite a normal scene in the Stanton household. He sensed that if he let the subject drop now he could never re-open it, yet confronted with the nearly tearful Peter he had no choice.

'I believe you,' he said gently, finally.

Isobel looked up at Peter. He stood by the desk, still holding the coin in a white-knuckled fist. Now he let the coin fall to the desk. The action relaxed him and he grinned awkwardly. Isobel felt a rush of relief.

# Five

'Round about here . . .'

'What do you mean, "round about here"?'

'It was sort of here – near here.'

'You're sure?'

Peter hesitated, then was honest. 'No. Not sure at all.'

The Professor was right at Peter's shoulder. Beyond him Peter could see the elderly single-decker bus that was to serve as the on-site HQ to the excavation. By it stood three men, all looking at Peter and Mr Stanton.

'Now wait a minute.' Mr Stanton put his hand on Peter's arm. 'You said there was no problem finding the exact place. You said you knew exactly where it was.'

'I know. That's what I thought.'

'You said you knew.'

'Well, I did – I do – but . . .'

'But what?'

'Everything looks the same – you know?'

'This is wonderful.' It was the opposite. The Professor was furious.

'I remember the sign.'

The M.O.D. sign leant wearily into the breeze that cooled the early morning air. Mr Stanton took a deep breath and expelled it slowly. 'It doesn't matter. It's my fault. I should have got you out here a week ago, with or without official approval. Never mind, we've got all the time in the world.' He knew how pressure could confuse the best memory. 'Look, I'll have a cup of tea with the boys. You just relax. Wander about a bit, get your bearings. There's no rush. OK?'

He managed a smile, and though Peter perfectly understood the motivation behind the words, he found they worked.

'Yeah. OK.'

Mr Stanton sauntered over to the waiting men by the bus. He spoke to them and they turned away and climbed up into the old coach. Mr Stanton waved at Peter and followed them in. They would be watching his every movement, Peter was sure.

In the bus, which had been stripped and fitted out rather haphazardly as a large caravan, Mr Stanton and his colleagues gazed out at Peter. He stood, undecided, for a long time.

Brian Vosper, the team's burly photographer and surveyor, was testy. 'First time I've started a dig like this.'

'It'll be all right,' said Mr Stanton.

'Yes? We might start work by tea time, might we? When do the pubs open round here?' Mr Stanton ignored him. 'Eleven o'clock? No – twelve, because it's Sunday. Thank you, Jim.'

'Shut up and make some tea.'

'I've had two cups already.'

They saw Peter walk over to the M.O.D. sign and look around. His eye-level took in the bus and he turned his back on it, looking out across the flat Romney fields below him.

'I was cross with him,' the Professor regretted.

'Good.'

'No, we're upsetting him. he can see us watching. We shouldn't look concerned.'

'I see. Act natural. I'm afraid I didn't bring a pack of cards. We could always play charades.'

'Just sit down and shut up for a minute.'

When Peter looked back at the bus he could see its occupants were no longer at the windows. Even so, he sensed attention was still on him. The rolling, hummocked ground appeared totally different from this angle. Perhaps he should re-enact the events of the evening on which he had made the discovery – take the route he had taken those days ago and let his feet, not his brain, lead him to the spot. Feeling acutely self-aware, he walked over to the garden fence of the big white house. Where exactly had he climbed over? Somewhere near the bottom of the garden . . . there, at that post where the fence was at its firmest. Should he start from the garden itself? He looked at the house. The picture windows reflected the morning sun; it was as if the house was blinded by the light: one could not see in and it seemed impossible that anyone could look out. But perhaps that was what someone *was* doing – looking out of one of the windows to catch Peter's act of trespass. He would start from this side of the fence.

'Good boy.' The Professor again had Peter under observation from the bus. Brian Vosper joined him.

'What?'

'He's retracing his steps. Starting from scratch. I should have thought of it myself, but I got cross instead.'

The two students who made up the rest of the archaeological advance party approached their seniors in the team. 'Any luck?' asked one. Mr Stanton held up a hand to command silence.

'What is this – a seance or something?' But, despite himself, Vosper felt the tension too.

Peter walked slowly and stiffly, uncoordinated by self consciousness. It wasn't working. Perhaps he was moving at the wrong pace. Certainly he was concentrating too hard. He simply didn't feel as he had that evening. Perhaps he had passed the place already. He stopped and looked at the bus. Four faces looked back at him. He continued walking, positive now that he would not remember where he had lain down. Wait a moment – it looked . . . just like all the others. He saw he had by now definitely come too far into the field and began to walk back doggedly towards the house, imagining derision in the bus.

Isobel had said she would come. He found himself wishing she was here already. He walked on. Oh no – he was almost back at the fence. A cloud passed across the sun and the windows of the white house darkened. There was a figure watching him from a room on the first floor. He couldn't make out whether it was a man or a woman, but there it sat, quite still, head turned in his direction. The cloud passed and sunlight again flashed from the glass of the windows, hiding the seated figure. Feeling like a criminal under surveillance from every side, Peter set off once more with his back to the house. Unconsciously he was moving faster, his mind absorbed in the memory of the figure in the window, and when he next took stock of his surroundings he stopped. The landscape was familiar again. He was within a few metres of his resting place on that strange evening. It was . . . between those evenly spaced hillocks – *there*. He waved to the bus.

'We have lift-off,' intoned the older of the two students, in a poor American accent.

'Maybe. Let's go, then.' The Professor led the general exodus from the bus.

As every step brought them closer to Peter, so they could see his sudden confidence seeping away. When they reached him, the Professor was determinedly cheerful.

'Well?'

Peter hung his head. 'I'm sorry. I thought I had it for a moment.'

'Oh, for heaven's sake!' The younger student fixed Peter with a look of plain contempt. Peter raised his eyes and the student's expression altered. Peter's stare was dispassionate and chilling. The student looked away. Peter spoke quietly to Mr Stanton.

'I'm sorry I can't do better for you. We're close here, anyway. I've got a line on it, kind of. The general area. I'm sure this time.'

'I didn't know what I'd started.'

Peter and Isobel were in the bus, working their way through a packet of biscuits. It had been a long time since breakfast. A hundred metres away, lines of string had been pegged into the ground, marking a boundary around several of the hummocks and mounds of earth. The Professor and the younger student were working at one end of the perimeter, digging carefully into one of the mounds, while Brian Vosper and the other student were equally busy at the other end, using trowel and penknife to cut into and sift the surface earth.

'Sondages. Sample cuts before they really get going. I told you it was boring.' Isobel looked sidelong at Peter. 'It'd be a great practical joke, wouldn't it?'

'What would?'

'To get a team of men grubbing about in the earth

for days and days when there really wasn't anything there.'

She wasn't serious; Peter knew her well enough by now. 'There *is* something there.'

'Yes, I know. But it'd be a good joke. They look so silly.'

Angus, the student working with Professor Stanton, talked as he pared away the earth.

I can't imagine why no one's tackled this place before. It's a natural. The whole thing looks like a burial ground, even to me. There must be aerial photographs of it. Anyone could see at a glance, couldn't they?'

The Professor sat back and rubbed a dirty knuckle across the corner of his eye. 'Didn't Brian tell you?'

'What? That it's been excavated before?'

'No. This glorious plot of land was used as a testing ground for landmines during the war.'

Angus stopped work at once. 'You're kidding.'

'No. That chucked things about a bit. Safe enough now, though, they tell me. Yes – look over to the edge of the escarpment. No mounds of earth. They wouldn't test there in case of a fall.'

They resumed work, turning over the grass and earth with their trowels, as the Professor continued: 'What must have happened when Peter made his find was that one or more of those explosions had thrown up stuff from deeper. I don't say it's not a burial ground, but if it were it would be some distance underneath.'

Angus scooped up half an inch of soil and ran his penknife through it with little optimism.

Peter lay on the floor of the bus, hands behind his

head. Isobel sat at a fold-away table, looking down at him.

'What does your father think about this?'

'Dad?' Peter was embarrassed. 'He doesn't know too much about it, actually. He knows I'm helping here, but . . .'

'You didn't tell him it was you who made the dig happen in the first place?'

'That's it. He's excited enough as it is. I asked your father not to tell him, either.'

'Why not?'

It was difficult. 'He . . . gets so worked up. It all gets to be about *him*, somehow. Like, well, say I'm picked for the football team. I tell Dad and he's off about how we used to have kick-abouts in the garden and how he's always encouraged me and coached me. It's all about him, not me. Then he comes along to the match, if he can, and he starts shouting – and he doesn't really know a thing about football – and everyone's looking. He wants to be proud of me. It puts you off. If I told him I'd found something archaeological, he'd be here every day like some sort of official observer. Calling the papers and stuff . . .'

'It's not just him is it? You don't want anyone to know.'

'No, I don't, as a matter of fact. I can do without the bother. I just want to be ordinary. Left alone.'

Peter got to his feet and sneezed. The floor of the bus was dusty. 'Actually, I kind of wish I hadn't found those things. Or anyway, that I'd just left them where they were.'

'That's crazy.'

'No it isn't. I don't think I like archaeology. I told your father that when I gave him the coin.'

'Did you?'

'I said it was like disturbing the dead, in a way. He said that was a contradiction in terms.'

'Just the kind of slick thing he would say.'

'He was all right about it. He just didn't understand.'

'Yes – that sounds like him, too.'

There was a lull in their talk as they watched the four archaeologists working as gingerly as though there were still live landmines in the field. The sun was beginning to slow-cook the bus, raising smells of metal and wood.

'Do you ever get the feeling you're being watched all the time?' Peter asked.

'No.'

'It's probably just me. This morning, with your father and the rest of them.'

'There'll be a few more out there if they turn anything up.'

'And there was somebody watching me from that big house.'

'Mrs Robertson, probably. The owner.'

'You know who lives there?'

'She's the one who gave Daddy permission to dig in Culver Wood. Only he's put it off because of your find here.'

'She gave her permission? How come?'

'It's hers. She owns it.'

It had never occurred to Peter that any one individual might actually own Culver Wood. It had always seemed that it was . . . what? Not *his*, exactly, but its own; 'private property' somehow belonging to no one. Perhaps Council land.

'I never knew that.'

'What's the matter?'

'Oh, I don't know. I go in there somethimes.'

'It says "private", doesn't it? Oh, I forgot. That doesn't worry you.'

'I go in there a lot, actually. It's really nice. Peaceful – you know.'

'What – like a special place to you?'

'I suppose so.' He didn't like the childish phrase 'special place'.

Isobel looked knowing. 'You didn't like the idea of Daddy digging there, did you?'

'Didn't I?'

'No.'

He smiled at her. 'Perhaps not.'

'Then you found those things, here, instead.' She was going to add *by coincidence,* but stopped herself. He changed the subject.

'The way you talk, it seems like you don't get on with your father.'

'No, I don't. Not really. Not at the moment.'

'I was thinking. It might be interesting if we had a look at Culver Wood. I mean, it'd be something to do.'

Their eyes met. Isobel was casual. 'It couldn't do any harm.'

'We could just have a look one day. Or night. Something to do.'

'What are you two going to do, then?'

'I don't know,' said Isobel.

The men were about to start their lunch in the bus. Bored, Peter and Isobel had already had theirs.

Brian Vosper lit his pipe, prompting the Professor to say, 'Well for goodness' sake get some fresh air. You've been in here all morning. Go for a ride on your bikes or something.'

'All right.' Isobel stood up.

'And if you come across a whole Roman legion sleeping in their breastplate don't bother to tell me about it, Peter. You've given us quite enough to do already.'

But it was said with a smile. Peter grinned back.

They stepped down from the coach on to the grass and walked away. As if by mutual consent they went down to the dig. It looked particularly small in the great tract of open ground, and the sun was at its brightest in the broad blue sky, seemingly intent on exposing to ridicule the team's efforts of the morning. The two mounds that had been the objects of attention had become earthy rather than grassy, that was all.

'Exciting, isn't it?' Isobel moved away. Peter remained looking at the ground that had been marked off. He had an idea that the hummock closest to the centre was the one. The rabbit holes looked right.

'Come on!' Isobel was waiting for him. No doubt he should tell her father . . . but they were having lunch now and of course he could be mistaken. Best avoid a fuss.

'Come on where?' He joined Isobel.

'I don't know.' She laughed, looking at him as she ran a hand through her hair.

Peter took charge. 'Let's have a look at the house.'

'It's a perfect position, isn't it?'

'What for?'

'For a house, stupid.' She laughed again.

'Yeah.' They walked towards the garden. 'That's Culver Wood, beyond it.'

From this far away it looked impenetrable. 'It's old, isn't it?'

'Do you want a look?'

'How?'

'Across the garden. The way I came.'

'Oh . . .'

'Come on. Trespass is my middle name.' He thought: *That'll stop her flirting.*

They rested their hands on the fence, taking the initial step that clarifies one's degree of resolve. The sloping lawn was bisected by a brick path running down from the house. On either side of the path were flower-beds and bushes. It had evidently been felt that trees would spoil the view. The sun no longer reflected from the windows and as far as they could see there was no one looking at them from the house.

'What do you think?' Isobel asked.

'Let's give it a go. She's probably having her lunch. We can come back by the road, if you're scared.'

'Who's scared?'

'Here we go, then. We'll just walk across normally.'

Peter scaled the fence first and, at Isobel's request, aided her over too.

'You don't need my help.'

'I do.'

'You don't.'

'What's the difference, anyway?'

They set off across the lawn. Peter pointed out the view of the Marsh and the Channel with proprietorial satisfaction. 'It's great, isn't it? You can see right across to France – see? On the horizon, the dark line?'

'I know. You can see it from where we were. It's no different.'

'It'd be a great place to live, though,here.'

*'Who are you?'* The voice was soft and the more startling for that. Isobel clutched at Peter's arm.

On the path, at the side of a dark-leaved magnolia bush, was a wheelchair. In it sat a woman wearing a white cardigan over a dark blue dress, a white silk headscarf and sunglasses. She spoke again.

'Who are you?'

Isobel found her voice. 'Is it Mrs Robertson?'

'That's who I am. Frances Robertson. Who are you?'

There was a whirring sound and the battery-powered wheelchair turned sharply and moved a few feet down the brick path towards them.

'Well?' Mrs Robertson held her head high as though disdaining to look at the interlopers, and Isobel realized that her father had not felt it necessary to tell her that the owner of Culver Wood was not only crippled, but blind.

'I'm Isobel Stanton. My father . . .'

'. . . Doesn't know you're here, I take it.' It was only when Mrs Robertson smiled that one saw she was a woman past middle age: her face became cross-hatched by tiny lines. 'Who is that with you?'

'A friend.'

'I didn't think it would be an enemy.'

Peter spoke up. 'I'm sorry, We shouldn't be here.'

'And who are *you*1?' The light voice was suddenly intense with curiosity.

'Peter. I'm . . . Peter.'

The curiosity withered as quickly as it had bloomed. 'And why are you here, you two?'

'No reason,' said Peter.

'I see. Like all young country people you just wander about making a nuisance of yourselves. Killing time.'

Isobel said, 'We're not doing any harm.'

'I don't suppose you're doing anything at all. Why should you? I never do. Would you like a cup of tea?'

Isobel glanced at Peter, and then felt guilty that they could communicate without Mrs Robertson's knowledge. She looked back at the blind woman and said, 'It would be very nice of you.'

'Yes, very nice – thanks very much,' Peter echoed with a friendly voice and an unfriendly look at Isobel.

'Follow me then.' The wheelchair swivelled with precision and began to trundle up to the house. Isobel caught it up and walked along beside Mrs Robertson; Peter trailed behind.

As they approached the house they saw a concrete ramp had been set into the steps leading up to the french windows of the drawing room. Deviating neither to the right nor the left, Mrs Robertson's wheelchair took the incline and stopped by the tall, closed windows. As she swivelled the chair, Peter overtook Isobel and said gruffly, 'I'll do it.'

'My house, I'll do it.' Mrs Robertson's stretching hand found the handle and she swung open first one door and then the other. The chair pivoted again and she glided in on to the parquet floor.

'In you come. Shut the windows, would you? It's not a warm house.'

Peter shut the windows. 'Done it.'

'I heard you,' said Mrs Robertson, dryly.

Peter and Isobel looked at each other and then around the room. The wallpaper was faded, giving its pattern of dog roses an autumnal effect. The furniture was modern, chosen more for comfort than appearance and clashing with the heavily-framed pictures of seascapes and sailing ships that hung everywhere on the walls of the once-formal room. The exception to the maritime rule was a small watercolour that had taken the place of a mirror over the mantelpiece, showing a black cat sitting in a field of flowers. It might have been copied from one of those greetings cards in which you are required to sign your name to a piece of defective poetry.

Mrs Robertson untied her headscarf, revealing fine white hair swept back into a bun. This she touched, reassuring herself it was still there and still tidy. Whatever her age might be – around sixty? – her voice had the soft clarity of a much younger woman.

'There. Looking my best, I trust.'

There was a silence. Isobel wondered: *What do we do about tea? Offer to make it? Watch her taking hours to do it? What?* By her side Peter was fuming with social unease.

'Do sit down. On the sofa, so I know where you are.'

They sat down, facing Mrs Robertson. Isobel watched and listened with incredulity as the old lady unclipped a two-way radio handset from the side of her wheelchair and pressed in a button on its side.

'I have two visitors. Might we have some tea, please?' She had difficulty in replacing the handset. 'I hope it's working . . . It's not that I can't make tea, but it takes such a time, and I can't be bothered. Age brings no privileges whatsoever, but money does. So I have what used to be called a manservant, who drives my apparently quite wonderful-looking car, of which he takes infinitely greater are than he does of me. I can't promise it will be good tea.' She smiled, and the wrinkles sprang into place.

Peter said, 'Someone who works for you! I suppose he does the garden and things, too?'

'So he tells me.'

Peter was thinking of the stranger in Culver Wood. That would be him – the manservant. It would be a relief to have that minor mystery solved. Mrs

Robertson went on: 'I'm not here much. I have a stuffy flat in London which suits me much better. The windows here make it so cold. Too many of them and too big. My father built the house, with a view to a view, as he used to say. He had a poor sense of humour and even poorer taste in paintings, as you'll have seen. He was in the Navy.' Apparently this adequately explained all her father's failings. 'The watercolour above the fireplace I did myself. I believe it showed promise. I was thirteen.

'It's quite good,' said Peter, without giving it a glance.

'Do you like it?' Mrs Robertson turned her head a fraction.

'Yes. It's very good,' Isobel replied perfectly.

'Yes. I wish I had done more, but . . . there it is. I can tell you only one advantage of being blind and lame. It's bizarre, but one has no fear. No joy, either, but no fear.' Mrs Robertson's clear, modulated phrasing gave the impression she was starring in a play she had written for herself.

Now it seemed it was someone else's turn to speak, so Isobel said, 'It was kind of you to give my father permission to excavate Culver Wood.'

' "Excavate" sounds rather wholesale, doesn't it? And now he chooses to dig elsewhere. Men are so fickle. But I liked him. He was very persuasive.' Abruptly: 'Do you like him?'

'I . . . er . . . admire him.'

'I don't suppose he likes *that* much.' Her own remark amused Mrs Robertson.

The sounds of rattling preceded the arrival of a tea trolley. The door opened and a dark-suited man backed into the room dragging the trolley. Peter waited to get a good look at him. The man pulled the tea trolley to the centre of the room and straightened up. He was too tall and too round-faced to be the man Peter had expected him to be. Peter frowned. The man frowned too, he had not thought the guests would be so young.

'We'll help ourselves, Harry. Thanks very much.'

'I had the kettle on anyway.' Harry gave his employer a short smile and left.

'Look after yourselves, will you? And me. The lemon tea is mine. There won't be any biscuits, as I didn't ask for any. Now tell me – Isobel. How did Harry look at me! Was he admiring?'

Mrs Robertson was both teasing and seeking an honest answer. It was an unfair combination. Isobel handed the lemon tea to her. 'Here. Well . . . he looked polite.'

'Polite?'

'Yes – you know – respectful.' That should be acceptable, Isobel thought.

'Oh.' Mrs Robertson was disappointed. 'One can't ask, normally. And I've always imagined a look of mute devotion. And you're Peter.' Again the darting attack, unsettling its target.

'Yes. That's me.'

'How old are you? No, you don't have to answer that. Between twelve and sixteen?'

'That's it.'

'You live locally?'

'Yup.'

'A local boy. Have you seen me before?'

'Nope.'

'Let me guess your surname . . . *Sadler.*'

Peter was taken aback. 'Ford.' He couldn't think of anything to add and took a sip of the weak, scented China tea Isobel had given him.

'Well, I could hardly expect to get it right, could I? You don't want to talk to me, I gather?'

'I don't really have anything to say.' The continuous inquisition was rude, Peter thought.

'You're a man of action, perhaps.'

'I don't know.'

Mrs Robertson turned roguish. 'I think you are!' The playfulness evaporated and she was reflective. 'How you must pity me.'

'Well, I'm sorry – sorry you can't see.'

'I'm sorry too . . . Do you want to know what happened to me?'

'Not if you don't want to tell us.' Peter was ungracious, unwilling to continue the conversation.

Disconcertingly, Mrs Robertson took off her dark glasses. Her heavy-lidded eyes were almost colourless. As if to compensate for this her voice became richer. 'I was a civilian casualty of the war. I was extremely lucky to survive at all. It was my terrible injuries that led me to my husband. He was the doctor put in charge of my progress to health. We married when I was eighteen. I think it was solely because I had money that he made his offer.'

Mrs Robertson turned her sightless eyes to the magnificent view that was denied her, while Peter and Isobel sat appalled at this uncalled-for revelation.

The silence grew in volume.

'Have you finished your tea?' Mrs Robertson asked.

'Yes.' Isobel was first in. 'Thank you very much, Mrs Robertson.'

'He was much older than me, and not well off himself. Quite a nice man, probably.'

'I suppose we'd better get going,' said Peter hurriedly, anxious to prevent more reminiscences.

Mrs Robertson became hearty. 'Yes. I mustn't keep

you. It was good to have you here. You can go out through the garden.'

At the windows Peter looked back. 'You didn't mind our being on your land?'

'Not at all. The monotony of my life calls for such intrusions from time to time. A very pleasant surprise.'

Isobel waited for Peter to open the french windows, but he hesitated a moment longer, until Mrs Robertson said slowly, 'You interest me . . . Peter . . .' Then he opened the windows quite fast.

'Goodbye,' said Isobel, feeling that someone should say it. Mrs Robertson did not answer and they went out on to the terrace. Peter closed the windows and they walked down the concrete ramp and on down the garden path.

# Six

Outside the house with a view, it was distinctly warmer. Both Peter and Isobel felt listless.

'That was creepy,' Peter said.

'Yes.'

'She didn't seem real, somehow. And it was like all she was saying all the time was "Don't feel sorry for me" and all you could think was "Well, I'm sorry, but I do feel sorry for you". '

'Yes, that's how I felt.'

They had reached the fence at the bottom of the garden, where they came to a stop. Beyond the fence the ground fell away steeply; they could not go on and neither now wished to continue their expedition to Culver Wood. The Professor's dig seemed a world away, now, too.

'Well,' said Peter, 'I think that'll about do me for today.'

They heard a shout of triumph from the old Army testing ground. 'I think they've found something,' said Peter without animation.

Isobel was equally restrained in her reaction. 'Probably.'

They began to walk towards the fence they had climbed over, their view of the site initially obscured by shrubbery. A baritone voice began to sing jerkily. 'On Mother Kelly's doorstep – down Paradise Row . . .' Peter and Isobel rounded the bushes and saw that in the field Professor Stanton and Brian Vosper were doing an improvised folk-dance by the side of the dig. It was the Professor who was singing.

'. . . Joe dreams about Molly . . .'

The two students stood some distance away, obviously grinning from ear to ear.

'She dreams about Joe . . .'

'Yes, they've found something. Look at the way he's carrying on,' said Isobel disapprovingly. They climbed back over the fence.

'Isobel! Peter! Come on!' The Professor's voice had the cutting edge of extreme excitement.

Revealed on Mr Stanton's now grimy palms, the object of the celebration looked fairly commonplace to Peter. A twin-bladed axe head of blackened, pitted iron, its interest was merely that it was recognizable for what it was.

'And here – show them, Brian.'

Brian Vosper's smile was reserved as he passed to Isobel a broken piece of stonework. He was confident that, to the ignorant, archaeological artifacts held limited appeal. To annoy her father, Isobel casually confirmed the opinion. 'Oh yes? What is it?'

'I'll give you a theory,' said Mr Stanton. 'A fragment of a broken coffin.'

'A stone coffin?' Peter was surprised.

'Certainly a stone coffin. It's what I'd expect to find. My hypothesis is that in this field is a grave or graveyard from the later period of the Roman occupation of Britain and that the grave or graves have been violently disturbed by the action of explosives – namely the landmines that were tested here.'

Isobel identified the assured tones of the television personality; it was as if her father was already rehearsing for his first interview. Now he adopted the easy familiarity he used, as she thought, to make people like him. 'Hey, Peter. Let's have a word.'

Mr Stanton absently gave the piece of stone to Angus, who looked sourly at Peter, perhaps envying him the attention he was getting from the great man. Uninvited, Isobel followed her father and Peter as they walked towards the bus.

'OK, Peter.' They stopped. Professor Stanton took from his pocket the gold coin of Theodosius. 'It's a miracle this wasn't found before. Well, now it is – officially found.' He held the coin out to Peter. 'So. Who found it?'

'Peter did,' said Isobel.

'He says he didn't.'

Peter took the coin. Its heavy weight gave it a familiarity, it seemed. 'You found it.' He handed it back.

'Done,' said Mr Stanton crisply. 'But if you want to change your mind any time, you've only to let me know and the credit will be yours.'

'Oh – right.'

'Good. We'll get on with it, then. D'you want to help? Or . . .'

'I said I'd be back around tea time. And, well, it's a bit boring.'

'What *are* you interested in, Peter? I'm curious.'

'The usual things. You know . . .'

'Do I? Perhaps I've forgotten. Like what?'

'It's none of your business, is it?' said Peter peacefully.

Mr Stanton laughed. 'You're absolutely right. See you, then.'

'See you.'

The Professor smiled at Peter and walked back to the site. The smile had not been entirely friendly.

'He thinks he's so clever. I think you're stupid.' After a moment's hesitation Isobel had trailed Peter towards the spot where his bicycle lay. 'That's what he wants – the glory all to himself'

Peter did not answer, and reaching his bike, pulled it upright and wheeled it across the bumpy ground towards the gate to the road. Isobel again hesitated, but left her bike where it was, almost running to catch Peter up.

'Really he's glad you're not going to be in on it.'

Peter marched on.

'He wanted you to say that. He's like Pontius Pilate, he wants to do the wrong thing and have clean hands, too.' Peter's silence spurred her to further vituperation. 'He's a bighead. Selfish. You can't trust him. Look at him. Full of himself.

Peter stopped with her, still some way from the gate, and looked back. The archaeologists were deep in conversation on the site. Now Brian Vosper began to pace around, dealing slow motion karate blows into the air, demonstrating how the site should be carved up for future exploration. Peter gazed at the activity and smiled. 'Your father's all right.'

'What?'

'He's OK. Count yourself lucky.' He continued wheeling the bike to the gate, and Isobel once more followed.

'Oh yes. Mr Wonderful – that's what he thinks, anyway.'

They reached the gate, which Peter opened one-handed. When he was sitting on his bike, he said thoughtfully, 'He really looks at you when you're talking to him.'

'Does he?'

'Yes. I know what it is. Your Dad thinks I know

something – something I'm not telling him – right? But it isn't true.' She did not answer and he went on, 'Still, he's a smart bloke . . .'

'Oh – smart. Yes – he's *that.*'

'So perhaps he's right and I'm wrong.'

He pedalled away, leaving Isobel wide-eyed and stranded by the side of the road.

At home it could have been any dead hour on any dead Sunday at any dead time of the year. Peter's parents were slumped on the sofa watching show jumping on the television, with the curtains closed to enhance the picture. Peter sat on the upright chair by the door and watched with them. His father managed a word or two, though his eyes remained on the set.

'Hello. Interesting, was it?'

Peter got up and went to the front of the television to take a crumbly slice of fruit cake from the plate on the coffee table. He plumped himself down on the arm of the sofa, beside his mother. 'Not very,' he said.

'Well . . .' The word was perhaps meant to preface some opinion on archaeology, but the sentence died in his father's mind before it reached his lips.

'The wall has been giving problems all day,' came from the television. A horse and rider approached the obstacle at an uncertain, jerky trot. The horse bunched the muscles in its haunches and jumped awkwardly, almost sideways, clearing the seemingly solid wall without dislodging a single brick. The rider was thrown forward on his mount's neck and recovered as applause rang out.

'I don't care what they say,' Mrs Ford announced. 'That's not skill – that's instinct.'

'Oh well done, Paddy!' the commentator called.

* * *

On impulse, Peter swerved across the main street of the village and came to a shuddering halt outside Parsons' Store. The afternoon was hot and he had been cycling fast on the way back from school.

Inside the little shop, the Calor gas heater was switched off for the warmer months and the cool, sweet smell of rising damp rose unchallenged. The Parsons' principal sales were of newpapers, bread and milk, and the thinly occupied shelves gave evidence that the shop survived only because there was no competition in the village.

Mr Parsons was talking to the Vicar, Mr Holroyd, who had a sliced loaf squashed under a bony arm. 'I've seen him on the telly. Can't remember what on.'

'A leading man in his field – or should I say presently in one of *our* fields,' the Vicar joked. 'Hello Peter.'

'Hello, Mr Holroyd. Can of lemonade, please.' He reluctantly parted with some loose change, which Mr Parsons took just as reluctantly. His attitude, as usual, suggested he was loath to part with any of his stock, as if the everyday articles were in some way irreplaceable.

'Doesn't Professor Stanton's daughter go to school with you?' Mr Holroyd asked.

'Yes, she does, actually.'

'Bright girl, is she? I suppose she would be, with a Dad like that, eh?'

Peter twisted away from the Vicar's gossipy curiosity and saw his answer through the windows of the shop. 'Why don't you ask her yourself, Mr Holroyd? She's hanging about outside.'

'Oh – is she? Yes. Well, I will then, Peter. Thank you, Parsons.'

'Any time, Vicars.' The joke was so old that neither

man smiled at it any more. Mr Holroyd, with his overlong, eager stride, quitted the shop and buttonholed Isobel on the pavement.

'Anything else you want?' Mr Parsons was anxious at all time to keep his shop clear of customers.

'No. Thanks very much.' Peter had no option but to join the other two outside.

'Yes, that's right,' Isobel was saying, blushing and then looking angrily at Peter.

'Enjoying it here?' Mr Holroyd continued.

'Oh yes.'

'And here's Peter. A heathen through and through – but friendly, isn't he?'

'Not always.'

'Oh – a quarrel. Well don't let me disturb you, um . . .?'

'Isobel.'

'Isobel. Good. Quarrel on, then.' And Mr Holroyd walked off with giant strides, unconscious he had fully repaid Peter for his rudeness in the shop.

Isobel accepted the vicar's parting advice. 'You've been avoiding me all day,' she accused.

'So?'

'Well, it's not very nice.'

'You're a leech, aren't you. Want some lemonade?' He popped the ring pull and offered the can to Isobel.

She took a sip. 'Thanks.'

'You know what the trouble with living in the country is?'

'No. What?' She gave the can back.

'It's too small.'

'How do you mean?'

'Well, there's you, for a start. Following me about.'

'So?'

He took no notice of the challenge. 'And there's the vicar. That was our vicar. Wants to know everything about everyone. And he does, too, I should think. Everyone knows everything about everyone else in the country. Whisper, whisper.' His bad temper evaporated. 'Come on, let's have a sit down.'

'Where?'

'Churchyard.'

'In a graveyard?'

'Why not? Let's leave the bikes – we can see them from there.' They started to cross the road.

'Wouldn't the Vicar mind?'

'Don't be silly.'

The church was Saxon, built low and strong. The graveyard around it was small; fully tenanted since the end of the last century. Peter and Isobel sat on the last resting place of Sarah Williams, 1802-1857, beloved wife of John. The stone catafalque was the height of a low sofa. Just above them a dark, grimly surviving yew tree stretched out its branches.

'I haven't been avoiding you, as it happens.'

'You have.'

'I've been thinking.' Peter began to think and Isobel let him. They watched a girl of about ten take her younger brother into Parsons' Store. The children came out with a single packet of crisps, which they shared on the spot as soon as they had been driven from the shop.

'I think – I don't know – ' said Peter suddenly, 'I think I've got an instinct for history. Does that make any sense?'

'I don't know.'

'Well, it's hard to explain. Maybe it's not always going to happen, but recently I've been . . .' *Seeing things*. He couldn't say that. 'I've been sensing things somehow. Like, say, that place I showed your father.' He wondered if this explanation would suffice. He did not want to go on to tell Isobel his suspicion that, when he had seen the Second World War aeroplane, he had been experiencing an actual vision from a former life. He generalized instead, voicing a fervent hope.

'Probably it's something that happens to quite a few people, but only at a certain time in their lives, and they don't take any notice of it; and then it goes, maybe, and they've never really known it was there. At least, they haven't taken it seriously.

'You've lost me.'

'Yes, well, I'm not surprised. Anyway, I'm only telling you because I wouldn't mind some help.'

'Help you? How?'

'Culver Wood.'

'Oh. Culver Wood,' Isobel said slowly.

'Well, your father thinks there's something there. Only, um . . .' Peter's eyes met Isobel's, 'he's busy somewhere else, isn't he, for a while?'

'Yes – that's right.' Isobel gave nothing away, leaving Peter to make the running.

'You're not exactly fond of him at the moment.'

'No, that's true.'

'So anyway, I'm going to have a look in Culver Wood. You remember Mrs Robertson – she said she didn't mind if we messed around on her land.'

'Oh, I see. You've been planning this.'

'Sort of, perhaps I have.' He stood up and leant against a thick branch of the yew tree. 'I thought you might be interested, anyway.'

'Why not Patel?'

'He's too practical. I don't want to be laughed at.'

'You don't think I'll laugh at you, then?'

'No, I don't.'

'Well, perhaps not.'

'I mean, the kids at school and everything, they think we're going out together anyway, so . . .' He noved further away from her, embarrassed. 'So what's the difference, if you know what I mean?' He added hurriedly, 'Anyway, it's something to do.'

'Yes. All right.' It was as simple as that, somehow.

'Great,' said Peter with relief. 'Look – I'll tell you – what with the dig being so close, we'd have to go at night. That's the problem. I'm not scared particularly, but we'd get more done – digging and that sort of thing – if there were two of us.'

'And whatever happens, we don't tell my father?'

'Well . . . See what's there first.'

'I can't get out at night. I don't think it would be easy.'

'If you don't think you can make it past him, you could ask him if you could put that tent on the lawn. Just for a night or two.'

'Oh, yes. Actually he might even be very pleased about that . . .'

'Give it a go, anyway.'

'What are we going to need?'

Patel said, 'He never was all that approachable, but now . . .'

'He's gone girl-crazy,' said Barry. 'It's always the hard men who fall the furthest. I should know.' He grinned at the Indian, who automatically curled his lip in disbelief. They had taken their attention from the kick-about for a moment and were watching Isobel and Peter, who were in earnest conversation by the gym building.

Isobel was excited. 'We'd have to make it some time

after midnight, to be sure he's asleep – but I honestly can't see a problem – he was really keen about the idea. I think.'

'Make it tomorrow night, then.'

'Oh. Yes. Why not?'

Leaving the house at one in the morning, Peter had a moment's guilt as he put up the snib to keep the door unlocked during his absence. The guilt passed very quickly. Above him, heavy, smoky clouds were drawn noiselessly across the night sky, smothering the moon. It was surprisingly warm.

As he rode towards the Stantons' house he regretted again that the clandestine nature of the expedition made it unwise to take tools of any kind other than the pitiful little garden trowel in the pocket of his anorak. He could imagine being questioned by a policeman: 'I see you're carrying a spade. Do you know what the time is?' As it was he felt obliged, on seeing the glow of distant headlights, to lay down both his bicycle and himself in a roadside ditch until the car had gone by. After that he put on speed.

He was prickly with warmth and breathing hard as he left his bike by the gate and walked cautiously up the path. Isobel's tent was a very visible shape on the lawn, for there was light shining dimly from the study window. Peter sneaked his way round the perimeter of the garden to get a look inside. The room itself was unlit: it was reflected light from the hall. Someone was standing just the other side of the window! Oh, of course, one of the wooden statues, all too human in the half light. He was exhaling with relief when a hand touched his shoulder and he felt his stomach revolve.

'It's all right,' Isobel whispered, 'he's asleep.'

'Oh thank you very much! That was a daft trick,' he hissed back.

'I've been waiting for hours.' She was dressed in jeans and a sweater and was petulant. 'It wasn't very nice. I felt nervous. Hang on, I'll get my bike.'

Isobel's admission that she was on edge gave Peter a feeling of confident leadership which lasted until the moment Culver Wood loomed into view. They dismounted and on Peter's advice left their bicycles in the field opposite the wood. Then they only had to cross the road, climb the barbed wire fence and . . .

'What are we looking for?'

'Whatever your Dad's looking for.'

'A Roman temple.'

'Well, that's it, then. We're looking for a Roman temple.' It seemed absurd. He wanted to call it all off.

Isobel took a rational approach. 'I suppose there'd only be a few remains. Bits of stone – that kind of thing. What do you think we'll find?'

'Absolutely nothing. Might as well be honest. It'd be a bit much to ask. We just stroll in and turn up a lost civilization. Probably there's nothing there. In any case, we've only got a couple of hours and – well – let's just call it a preliminary examination. It's only a bit of fun, anyway, really.'

They crossed the road, almost relieved at the idea there was nothing to find in Culver Wood.

'Hey – look what I've found.'

'What? Where?'

'Over here – where do you think?' Peter waved the beam of his torch and Isobel's torch wended its way through the trees to join him, followed by the dark shape of the girl herself.

'What is it?'

'Look. Chaffinch egg. Broken now, of course.'

'Is that all? Are they rare?'

'No, I don't think so.'

'Terrific,' said Isobel sarcastically. 'That makes it all worthwhile, doesn't it? I'm going to be a wreck in the morning and all we find is an old bird's egg.'

'Well, it's a big place. We don't even know where to start looking. And it's hard to get your bearings in the dark.'

By now the wood seemed an old frined, but caution kept their voices low. 'Why don't you use your famous instinct?'

'All right – no need to be like that.'

'Or use some logic. If you built a temple, where would you put it?'

'Easy. This was once a cliff, right? I'd put it looking out over the sea. Near the edge.'

They were quiet for a moment, then Isobel voiced their common thought. 'Well, it's worth a try. Which way?'

'We haven't come too far in yet, so I know roughly where we are, I think. Best go round the outside, if we want to be sure.'

As they worked their way around the wood they could see the pale outline of Mrs Robertson's house through the trees. Behind Peter, Isobel stumbled.

'Careful. Nearly there. It's tremendous in the daytime – looking out from here.'

They could feel the night breeze on their faces. Peter took Isobel's hand and led her to the last of the trees, where the land fell away. Isobel felt a return of her nervousness. 'It's safe, isn't it?'

'Sure. Anyway, we won't be searching right on the cliff top. A little way back in . . . say – here.'

The impossibility of their task again struck them as

Peter began to scrape at the ground with the trowel. 'All right – I know it's no use – but we're here now, so . . .'

They both trained their torches on the mossy ground by the roots of one of the beech trees. Working with a little care, they cleared the topsoil from an area of a few square metres, then rested for a minute, looking at the ugly mess they had made.

'What kind of torch is that?' Peter asked.

'I don't know. Ordinary. Batteries – you know.'

'Turn it off a minute.'

Isobel complied. Peter switched off his torch, too.

'What's up?' said Isobel.

'Can you hear something?'

'Like what?'

'I thought it might be your torch. A kind of humming.'

'No, I don't hear anything.'

Sitting in the dark, silent, their senses were sharpened.

'Oh,' Isobel whispered. 'Yes . . .'

So deep as to resemble the bass notes of a church organ, they heard what sounded like a sustained musical chord. The ground was alive with the low sound, as though an electric current were passing through it. Barely perceptibly, higher notes crept into the harmony. It was as if a boy chorister had joined in with a voice of clean spring water, free of feeling yet stirring the emotions. Other notes now blended in until the effect was of human voices imitating a spinning top with a densely woven, continuous humming. The sounds were too attractive to be frightening and so faint that it was hard to tell the exact moment when they stopped.

Peter breathed out audibly. 'What was *that?*'

'Wait.'

The high, clear voice sang a few notes more, under which the vibrating bass came in as support. The bass notes faded. The higher notes ceased with finality.

'Quick,' Peter said urgently. 'Quick.' He got up and began to move into the wood.

'No.'

'Come *on*.'

'No.'

'I'll leave you here,' Peter threatened. 'I'll go by myself. This is what we came for; no wonder there are stories about this place. Get up!' He pulled Isobel to her feet. 'Don't turn your torch on. We won't be caught, if we're careful.'

'Caught?' The word froze Isobel again, but to keep her balance she had to go where Peter pulled her. They moved almost silently, feeling their way among the giant trees. It seemed to Isobel that the wood had grown still bigger in the darkness: they inched onwards for what felt like whole minutes. Then Peter tightened his grip on her arm. They stopped.

Directly ahead of them the trees could be seen more clearly, touched by a deep red light. Somewhere farther on into the wood there must be the source of this ominous light, which ebbed and flowed much as though a door were being opened and closed on a room in which a fire was burning. The trees became as indistinct as the others around Peter and Isobel. The event, whatever it might have been, was over.

'Oh no,' Peter murmured. 'Back! Back!'

Isobel obeyed without question. Their progress was loud as they floundered back towards the old cliff. Realising this, Peter tugged Isobel to a halt. His voice barely carried to her. 'Quiet. We must be quiet. We can't be seen but we can't see anything or anyone ourselves. So we're quiet – all right?'

Thereafter the journey was delicate and agonizingly prolonged. Around them was a listening silence: they heard no sounds of pursuit.

At last they could see between the trees the paler light of open spaces. They felt their way to the last trees before the long drop down and Peter at last relaxed his hold on Isobel's arm. It felt bruised.

They sank to the ground. Isobel's voice trembled. 'What are we doing here?'

'If there're people back there, they're going to be leaving the wood. Well, there's no way out this way, is there?'

Put like that it was not entirely reassuring. 'We'll be all right here,' he said firmly. He was beginning to think his retreat had perhaps been prompted more by regret that he had brought Isobel than fear for himself – though there was no doubt the sounds had made him very nervous.

'How long – how long do we stay?' Isobel whispered.

'Till it begins to be light. But from now on, no noise – no talk. I'm not taking any chances.

Isobel could see he was making himself comfortable, pushing his back up against a massive tree trunk so that the tree became a tall-backed chair. She edged over to him. He put out a hand and she took it.

# Seven

'Time to go.'

He nudged Isobel, who had collapsed against him.

'Wake up. Time to go.'

'Oh . . . Yes . . .'

Dawn was fading up, bringing to the fields below them the cold reality of a neon light.

'Everything's all right?' Isobel asked vaguely.

'Of course it is.'

She disengaged herself from him and stood up stiffly. Peter had even more trouble getting to his feet. He was short tempered and brusque. 'Just time to have a look.'

Isobel's quiet compliance as she followed him back through the trees showed that she too was having second thoughts about their flight those hours ago.

Culver Wood was benign again.

They wandered about for a while and stopped momentarily in Peter's clearing, which looked as undisturbed as the rest of the wood. Peter scuffed at the ground with his foot. 'I don't know,' he said. 'Could have been a courting couple.'

'Oh come on. Those sounds – what about *that*?'

'Radio? Cassette player?' It was hard to recall the faint noises at this distance of time.

'And that light?'

'Someone playing tricks? I don't know. Could have been anything. We didn't get close enough.'

'I didn't want to.' Isobel spoke with feeling.

'Yes – that's right – you didn't.'

'Nor did you.'

With silent honesty Peter did not argue. 'Better get a move on. If your Dad catches you, you tell him you went for a morning ride. That's what I'm going to do if they see me.' Then he spoke urgently. 'I'm not going to tell *anyone* about what happened.' For no reason he could define, Isobel's silence on the matter seemed incredibly important and he waited anxiously for her response.

'I don't suppose I will, either. We'd only get laughed at.'

'Yes.' Yes – of course. That was the reason.

They made their way to the road and climbed the barbed wire fence. As they were about to cross the road, Peter said quietly: 'Just act normal. Let's get over the road and get the bikes.'

'What is it?' Isobel followed his gaze down the road. About fifty metres away, walking towards them, was a small man wearing a tweed hat and a dark pullover.

They ignored the approaching figure and reclaimed the bicycles. The metal frames were wet and cold to the touch. Peter heaved them over the fence to the waiting Isobel, then climbed back over himself. The man was close now; his shoes crunched down on the road in a regular, unhurried rhythm. Peter and Isobel mounted their bicycles with their backs to him.

The footsteps stopped.

Drawn by the quiet, Peter twisted round in the saddle. Isobel looked back too. The man took a few more steps towards them. His voice was soft and halting, at odds with his stern face.

'Up . . . early, aren't you?'

'That's right,' Peter said with light indifference. 'So are you, if it comes to that.'

A bleak smile touched the man's mouth and then his dark eyes locked on to Isobel's. 'You . . . should be careful, the company you keep.'

Isobel made no reply, transfixed by the steady stare.

A blackbird or thrush called questioningly from Culver Wood, exploring its vocal abilities after a night's rest.

'I'd keep away . . . from him, if I were you.'

It seemed the man might have added more, but he only nodded and moved on past them down the road. Once his eyes were hidden from them, Peter and Isobel relaxed. From the back he looked as harmless as anyone could. They watched him until he was out of earshot, then Isobel turned to Peter.

'Who was that? Do you know him?'

'No. Some weirdo.'

'I'm glad he's going in your direction, not mine.'

'He doesn't worry me. Look – I'll be round this evening. We'll talk it all over. All right?'

'All right.' She hesitated, looking after the receding figure of the strange man.

'Off you go, then.'

'Why don't we just forget about it all?'

'Well – perhaps we will. But we'll talk it over first. OK? See you later. Quite soon, actually.' He grinned and Isobel felt better.

'See you later.' She bicycled off, an increasingly small part of the landscape; easy to feel sorry for simply because she was alone. Peter wondered if he would have time for breakfast at home. He turned and saw the stranger in the distance, no longer walking but standing by a gate to a field, waiting. Well, so what.

Peter cycled leisurely along the road. The man watched him every second of the way. As he drew near, Peter slowed to a halt. All right, if this odd bloke had anything to say, let him say it. Had he been in the wood last night? Even if he had, he could not know Peter and Isobel had been there to see or hear anything.

They surveyed one another. The man had nothing to say. When the staring silence became too uncomfortable for Peter, he broke it.

'What are you doing around here?'

The reply was almost whispered. 'I could . . . ask you that.'

'Come on. What are you doing hanging around the wood?'

There was another silence and Peter was about to repeat his question, when the stranger answered him.

'You don't know?'

'How could I know? Know what? Were you in the wood last night?'

'Were *you*?' The man's eyes glittered with interest and Peter began to feel very unconfident.

'Oh, forget it!' he said, trying to sound contemptuous. 'Forget it.'

He rode on, feeling the full power of the man's attention on him, tracking him down the road with those fact-recording, uncompassionate eyes.

The sitting room in the Stantons' house had that indefinable lack of cheer that rooms gather to themselves when they are little used. Two beige sofas faced each other across a steel-framed glass coffee table; the other furnishings stood tight against the walls in a conspicuously unimaginative use of the space. The dark floorboards were highly polished and so slippery that the large, vivid Mexican rug slid as you stepped on to it. The portable television set in one corner had the look of an afterthought – after as little thought as possible had been given to the arrangement of the room.

The school day had been over for some time, but Peter had arrived from home only a few minutes ago. Sitting beside him on one of the sofas, Isobel yawned and leant back, stretching out her hands until they trembled with the effort.

'Lord of Light. Mithras was known as the Lord of Light.'

'Wait a minute. Just supposing—' Peter checked himself, but the idea still seemed valid. 'Just supposing there still is a cult around Mithras. I mean – some people go around being Druids even now. So why not? Just suppose there's this sect, or whatever, and they're worshipping Mithras and he's the Lord of Light – couldn't that explain the light we saw? Something symbolic, it might be.'

Isobel was dubious. '*Might* be.'

'It makes sense of it, anyway. The music and the light.'

'There's no mention in the books about anyone still believing in him. "The Unconquered God, a man hewn from the living rock." If you believe that you'll believe anything. There's hundreds of funny religions around.'

Professor Stanton popped his head round the door. Peter almost jumped.

'You two all right?'

'Oh yes. Fine,' Isobel answered.

'Not telly-watching?'
'Not yet.'
'Wonders will never cease.'
'Have you found anything more yet?' Peter asked.
Mr Stanton gave him a look that was hard to read. 'Not yet. Early days, though.'
He disappeared back into his study. Isobel waited until they heard his door shut.
'Look. You've lived here all your life – you know the people around here.'
'So?'
'So how come you've never even heard a whisper about a secret cult?'
'Don't be soft. Because it's secret. Besides, I don't know everyone around here. That bloke we saw this morning – I've no idea who he is, for instance.'
He fell silent.
'Do you think he could have had anything to do with all that stuff last night?' Isobel asked.
'I honestly don't know. It's possible, I suppose. He made me feel really uncomfortable, I know that much. How about you – what do you think?'
'I think we were tired and a bit frightened – at least, I was. And we're making a big deal out of something that'd have a pretty ordinary explanation, if we knew enough about it. We'll probably see something about something in the local papers and then we'll feel silly. That's the way things happen.'
'Perhaps you're right.' It had been a long day and Peter was suddenly exhausted. The adrenalin that had kept him going ran out of him like sand on hearing Isobel's prosaic attitude to their adventure.
'All the same,' he said wearily, 'I'm going back to the wood.
'I'm not.'

'So how will you ever know if —?'

Mrs Davies, without whom the Stanton establishment could not function, interrupted Peter by coming in with a plate of sandwiches.

'Something to keep you going. You know about supper, Isobel, love?'

'You've left a piece of paper.'

'I've left a lot more than that. You have to remember to preheat the oven. Don't forget, now. I don't trust your father, when it comes to—'

'It's all in the note, isn't it?'

'Yes. Well, I won't disturb you any longer, then.' Mrs Davies was hurt. She put down the plte of sandwiches and recovered her self esteem with, 'There's enough there to feed an army. Should keep you going.

'Thanks very much,' Peter said. He got up and took one of the sandwiches at random. Cheese and tomato. Not too bad. Eating the sandwich, he wandered to the window, waiting for Mrs Davies to leave. Outside, the orchard was like a picture. On the planned ranks of apple trees the neat, fresh green leaves were evenly distributed; the blossom had come and gone and the grass between the trees was pristine, cropped short.

'Why do I bother to feed you, if you won't eat?'

The question dragged his attention back to Mrs Davies, who had only to step into the orchard to complete a postcard for the tourists. She was plump, with pink, butcher's forearms bursting from the short sleeves of her brightly patterned acrylic dress. Isobel treated the question with mute contempt and Mrs Davies turned to leave.

'Thinking of your figure, I suppose.'

She walked to the door with dignity. Peter noticed how her dress was stretched across her broad back.

His head throbbed violently and deep in his brain there was a light *crack* as though a strand of wire had parted. Mrs Davies reached the door and –.

– he was running. Through trees. He felt branches tear at his hands and face. He could see the soft greens and gold of sunlight in a wood and could feel his pounding feet crushing down on to loose earth, scattering it noisily. Rising up around him, he could even smell the warm decay of the woodland floor. His chest hurt with the effort of breathing. He had obviously been running for at least several minutes.

He must stop. He must think. Was this reality, or. . . ?

He couldn't stop. The body that felt his in every muscle and sinew refused his wish and careered on through the trees. It was a dream, an hallucination, a memory.

It wasn't. Suddenly his right knee was lacerated by an abrasive tree trunk and the body that was his, but beyond his control, stopped – and he was looking down at the blood seeping from a broad graze on his naked knee. He saw he was wearing coarse, brown knee breeches and heavy shoes on his bare feet. He was conscious that his feet were sweating and raw inside their casings of stiff leather. Above the breeches he had on some kind of baggy shirt, stained and dirty. He could feel the constriction of a handkerchief knotted around his throat.

His body moved on without his bidding, as if it were an animal and he somehow contained within it. He was limping now, yet still moving as fast as he could. Although his painful haste suggested desperate flight, he himself felt little fear. It was hugely frustrating to be excluded from the emotion, thoughts and motives of the person in whom he was imprisoned in this otherwise wholly three-dimensional way. He *was* this person in all but his conscious mind. Peter knew: *It's me. Me in a previous existence. But when? And who am I?*

An unwilling passenger in his own body, he blundered onwards until at last the trees thinned and he felt himself slow to a more normal pace. It was evident from his every movement that he was now trying, as far as his injury would allow, to imitate a casual stroll when he left the protective cover of the wood. He limped out from the trees into a vast expanse of meadow and his sudden caution, for that was what it had been, proved justified. He saw, with a little shock of recognition, that he had arrived at some point along the old sea cliff. Two hundred metres away, beyond a dusty roadway of bare earth, the edge of the inland cliff was almost completely hidden by a long line of people who stood with their backs to him facing out over the lowlands and the Channel. At most points the line was at least three deep.

A jolting, syncopated sound made him look down the dusty road. Two barrel-bellied chestnut horses were drawing a carriage in his direction at a lively trot. The fat coachman's blue coat was layered with a series of heavy shoulder capes and even at this distance it was possible to see that the coat had many more metal buttons than could ever have a practical use. He wore a cocked hat with so much silver braid on it that it seemed he could only have hired it to play a pirate in a pantomime.

Still Peter was not scared, only overwhelmingly confused. His head was close to bursting with anxiety. In the midst of his confusion he had the idea his eyesight had miraculously improved, the images in front of him, all around him, were so distinct. His head began to ache again and he found himself thinking, quite dispassionately, *It's the air. It's clearer, somehow. It's unbelievably clear – that's what it is.*

Within his headache there was another sensation of something snapping and –

Mrs Davies reached the door and the patterned dress wrinkled on her shoulders as she turned to say, 'I'll see you tomorrow, love.'

The room was as real as had been the woodland and the old sea cliff. Peter realized he was still eating the cheese and tomato sandwich.

'When are you going back, them?' Isobel asked after the door had closed.

'What?'

'When are you going back to Culver Wood?'

'I . . . I don't know.'

His head was humming. The room contracted in around him and retreated to its normal proportions. But it was indistinct now, as though dusk had fallen.

His voice sounded faint, too. 'Isobel . . .'

*Snap.*

Here time had apparently passed.

He was forcing his way to the front of the crowd assembled on the cliff. He found his hand was pushing into the back of a squat man who was dressed, ascendingly, in buckled shoes and wrinkled red stockings under a pair of black breeches; while over a linen-backed waistcoat was strapped a soft leather apron which was showing the light-brown-sawdust look of much wear. The back of his head was badly shaved. It looked like a mushroom, stuck full of lead pencil points.

The man turned to investigate the pressure on his spine and Peter found himself looking into a pair of the brightest blue eyes – nearly on a level with his own.

'Hungry for a look at Boney?'

Peter hardly took in the words at first. He had become aware that his sense of smell was hard at work. The people around him had a sweet, heavy, farmyard smell; not unpleasant in the open air. He could smell spirits on the man's breath, too. This was hardly a dream. The man was friendly and his familiar Kentish accent made Peter feel less uncomfortable than might have been the case.

'You feel the wind on our backs? God's wind, they call it. Don't feel much, do it? There's more of 'em yet today. Be over soon, wind or no wind. And one night we'll see the beacons all ablaze all along the coast and I'll go down to the forge and cast something sharp right quick.'

The man smiled and Peter felt his face return the smile before he stepped forward to the grassy extremity of the cliff. He was more at one with his body now; in agreement with the moves it made. A reason came to him as to why he had forced his way to the front of the crowd: it might well be to hide more effectively from pursuit.

It didn't seem important as he stared out over the flatlands and on over the straits of Dover to France. The sweep of land beneath him appeared larger through lack of substantial buildings. To his left the sprawling urban mass that was Hythe was reduced to the size of a small fishing town. The wind ruffled Peter's hair and blew gently on the back of his neck. In the clear, clean air, France seemed several miles closer. One could distinguish colours and even the irregular, dark outline that must be the town of Boulogne.

Opposite the watchers of Kent, a great encampment littered the cliffs and beaches of France. The tiny French houses gave an indication of the magnitude of the military force, which could be contained only under the canvas of countless tents. Beyond the tents he could see a wood and – yes – that was the spire of a church. As he watched, squinting to focus his eyes, he could actually see the minute moving thread that was a long troop of cavalry jingling into the camp from the direction of Boulogne. Jingling? That sight was so vivid, although in miniature, that one could readily imagine the noises of hooves on earth, metal on metal, and the creak of equestrian leather. The horses would be huffing and blowing impatiently, as eager as their riders to be at the gallop, cutting through the defensive positions of the English.

He looked downwards again. What defensive positions? A feature of the Kent coast was the placement along it of the old Martello Towers, the small, rounded forts built to withstand invasion in the Napoleonic wars. Anywhere along this stretch of coast you would see at least one or two; and there had originally been many more of these gargantuan upturned flower-pots. Now, when they were most needed, none. Peter's small knowledge of the period led him to believe that, as he stood here on the old sea cliff in the ranks of the quaintly garbed country folk, he was in the first years of the nineteenth century. Who had instigated the defences here? Pitt the Younger. Prime Minister from 1804 until . . .

As he looked down, as people will, at the long drop beneath his feet, he saw that another defensive feature had not yet been established. Sheep were browsing where the Royal Military Canal should be: the waterway that, although narrow, made a peninsula of the whole of the land reclaimed from the sea; the entire Romney Marsh. The complete lack of deterrents to invasion suggested that the massive French force had only to effect a landing, and thereafter the revolutionary army could surge up through the country with ease, a true tide of destruction. And at this point England was without allies, standing alone against Napoleon.

Almost as if the eyes that were his but were not had become willing to obey his instincts, Peter found he had raised his gaze again to the French coast. All around him it was quiet except for a murmur of conversation from his left and, as he watched the French cavalry wending into the great camp, he no longer had the inclination to imagine the sounds of their progress. There, with a wood behind them, were thousands of French soldiers, and here, with a wood behind them, were a couple of hundred English country folk. It was an alarming mirror image.

But it had never happened. As before and afterwards in the history of England, the great invasion had never taken place. It wouldn't happen. It didn't happen. So the anxiety he felt had nothing to do with Bonaparte. Instead it centred on his unaccountable presence in this segment of time and the certainty that he was meant to be running from something. He mustn't stay here. Men were after him and if they caught him the consequences would be . . . Here he was at a loss. The motive for flight and the outcome of capture were beyond him. At any rate, he was relieved he now had some share in the working of this body and mind in which he was trapped. He began to wonder why he was not using the cover, provided by the crowd to get to some safer spot – if there was one.

Perhaps the same thought spurred the other Peter, the one in charge of their body. He was turning to go now. Beside him the smith – if so he was – spoke again.

'Seen enough to keep you quaking, have you?' He smiled and his eyes narrowed in infectious enjoyment. Then the smile fixed itself into his red face; his eyes dulled with vague suspicion or, perhaps, recognition. All of a sudden he looked sly. Peter felt nervous.

*Snap*. It was dark.

It was dark. In place of the smith's blue eyes was the black lift-latch of an unpainted wooden door. Peter was horrified that this latest whiplash transition had not brought him back to the Stanton sitting room.

He saw and heard the latch lifted and the top half of the door opened while the bottom half remained in place, like a stable door. Light and a waft of fetid air struck Peter in the face; a smell compounding smoke, vegetables, cooking and unwashed clothing. He blinked as the door swung wide and another pair of eyes stared into his.

'By God, Jem, you're in the wrong place here.'

Instinctively in tune with the action, Peter glanced behind him. No one was in sight and he had time to see a rolling field of young corn, strangely fluorescent in the moonlight, before his head turned back to see his friend – as he assumed the man to be – hastily unbolting the lower door. The man dragged Peter into the single room of the dwelling and turned to shut out the night with shaking hands.

There was not a single article in the room that

could have been anything but hand-made. A wood fire glowed in the wide hearth, the only source of light in the room, disturbing the shadows it had itself made. A misshapen straw mattress lay against one whitewashed wall; a low, splintered splay-legged table, absurdly reminding Peter of a coffee table, faced the fire along with a high-backed chair and a three-legged stool. There was an earthenware bowl on the table and by it a sodden hunk of bread. Peter's skin prickled with the heat; it was an odd time of year in which to have a fire. The man had to cook, of course . . .

'You sit down. There's food there. You're welcome, you know that.'

The food that was left consisted of a single potato beached in the shallows of some gravy, and that very second-hand bred. It was no surprise to realize that he was hungry. He was glad to sit down, too, and pulled the stool in towards the table.

'No – no. You take the chair. Sit you in the chair, Jem. You're in need of the rest.'

Jem. That was who he was, was it? He did as he was bid, discovering that he looked closely at the man, perhaps suspecting this degree of hospitality.

The man watched Peter eat. The potato was sweet and wazy. The bread made him choke; the yeasty crumbs clogged his mouth and throat. He was keeping his eyes on the man across the table, who was a stringy type, looking faintly ludicrous in a grubby smock. His dark complexion and unruly black hair led Peter to believc he must have Romany origins. The face was narrow, with the moistly apprehensive eyes of a spaniel. Peter wondered how many friends he – Jem – had in this time and place. Not many if this was the best he could do in times of trouble.

As if reading Peter's thoughts, the man reassured him.

'Have no fears. They've been here already.' He looked nervous. 'You make me wonder . . . what it is you have in mind this time.'

There now came the strangest experience yet in Peter's entrapment in the body that might have been his those many years ago. He spoke. With no control over what it was that was said. The voice vibrated in his throat and chest, a strong Kentish sound. It was as though he were a mute ventriloquist inside his own dummy, which could speak of its own voliton.

'I drew them away then came back. They'll not look for me so close to home.'

'You say that – yes – but what are you going to do? There's no staying here.' The man's imploring eyes added *'please'*.

'I could enlist.' Again the words arrived without thought.

'You're not seventeen.'

'The Navy, they would take me.'

'They would take any man.'

'I'd be wisest to go to Portsmouth. I'd be a foreigner there.'

'You might find it difficult to quit this part of the country.'

'I can't see why.'

'This. This is why.'

The man went to the straw mattress in the corner and took from under it a sheet of newspaper.

'You know, Jem, there's the Militia now. They've not much to do with themselves.' He spoke with contempt. 'And there's this, like I said.'

It was a crumpled page from the *Kentish Gazette*. Peter took in the date with a lack of surprise that was in itself surprising. June 12th, 1803. His eyes passed over a headline, BEACONS ESTABLISHED, as his friend pointed out, with a dirty fingernail, some lines at the bottom of the page.

ABSCONDED

*From service on this last Wednesday, Jeremiah Swan, apprentice miller, aged about fourteen. This being his second such offence his Master will give to any person the sum of one guinea on his being taken and brought to Deft's mill at Ruckinge. The Runaway has pale hair and on him a loose shirt and breeches, without waistcoat.*

It didn't seem such a terrible crime. Yet the lanky individual beside him looked smugly solemn when Peter glanced up at him. Presumably a guinea was a lot of money to most men in these days. The smith, earlier, might well have seen this advertisement; it would explain his altered expression.

He felt himself say, 'It goes against me, doesn't it?'

'He's hard, is old Deft. He'll have you, boy.'

Peter wanted to ask '*And what would happen then?*' He could not motivate his voice to say the words and found himself nodding and saying instead: 'He'd like to. I'll travel by night. Start out now. How did you come by this?' He meant the newspaper.

'Deft. He give them to folk all around. Says he can make life bitter for us, if he should care to.'

'I won't tell, Tom.' So that was his name.

'You're a good lad. Should never have gone to him.'

Peter's shoulders lifted in a shrug. 'It's all one, now.'

He got to his feet and his head spun. He thought: *Here I go again.* Nothing happened. His hand stretched out to Tom, who took it.

'You remember me, then, Tom. We'll not meet again.'

'Goodbye, young Jem. You mind after yourself.'

The two windows were shuttered. Peter – or, rather, Jem – was taking a last look around the meagre cottage. The fire had burnt down and the room was darker. He wished there had been more to eat. In the mind of Peter, if not Jem, hunger outweighed all else. He lifted the latch to the upper door and swung the heavy partition outwards.

Burning torches swayed in the night air. A large figure stepped sideways into vision.

'I cautioned you on many an occasion, Master Swan. You've nobody but yourself to thank.'

Under what looked for all the world like a modern top hat, Mr Deft's face was bulged and knotted by intense gratification. His lumpy features were doughy, as though he was a partially-baked product of his own flour, into which a knife had been prodded to make rudimentary slits for eyes.

Peter stood just where he was, looking now beyond the miller. Faces, none friendly, perhaps embarrassed, stared back. By the light of one torch, held by an elderly man in a long coat (were these men members of the local militia?), Peter saw a face he knew. It was not until then that he felt real fear for himself – Peter.

It was the man from Culver Wood.

This could only be a nightmare. Here the man wore a black waistcoat over a grey shirt and breeches, but the face, with its deep-set, unfathomable eyes, was unmistakable.

The sudden transition accomplished itself smoothly this time.

# Eight

'What?'

'Sorry?'

'What?'

'What do you mean, "what"?'

'You were going to say something.' Isobel appeared only mildly puzzled. She was eating a sandwich and there were minute crumbs in the corners of her mouth.

Peter licked his lips. 'I'm thirsty.' He was.

'Typical of that woman. Nothing to drink. What shall we have? Shall I make tea?'

'No . . . no . . .' What were they doing, talking about tea? His legs were shaking. He went to put the unfinished sandwich down on the coffee table.

'They're not very nice, are they?' Isobel said smugly. He noticed she went right on eating, however. Suddenly he couldn't stand her: she irritated him beyond reason.

'Oh shut up, for heaven's sake.'

'What have I done?' She was truly bewildered. The hurt on her face irritated him further.

'Nothing, nothing. I want to think, that's all.'

'What about?'

All she could do was ask questions. *About the fact I've gone mad or something. About the fact that while you've been sitting here filling your face . . .*

'What about? Tell me.' Now she was flirtatious

again. He couldn't deal with that. Peter tried to clear his thoughts. It seemed tremendously important she shouldn't know anything was wrong. Best just . . .

Her voice drove into his confusion. 'Tell me.'

'Oh, I don't know . . .'

'You're so mysterious, aren't you? The strong silent man with a face like a football.' Now she was bad-tempered.

'Oh yeah – very funny. Very good, that.' He was completely enervated. He didn't know how he'd manage the ride home; he didn't want to pass out. Words came to him. 'You want to know what I was thinking?'

'Yes – why not?'

To his own ear his voice was high, strained through a wire mesh of tension or hysteria. 'I was thinking that if I was to go back into Culver Wood again, there's no reason at all why I couldn't go in daytime – in broad daylight. No reason why *we* shouldn't go in the daytime. That's what I was thinking.

It might serve to shut her up. And it was true that Culver Wood was at the centre of all his recent experiences, somehow. Admitting the truth to himself, he now knew it was he that was scared of the wood; he that would not venture back alone, at any time of day. He avoided further thought on the matter, concentrating instead on the reality around him. It was a mistake. The subtly cheerless room, the floorboards beneath him, rendering up a smell of scented polish, were no more and no less of plain, factual existence than had been his conversation with the smith or the dying fire in the cottage. If anything, the room where he now stood was the more unreal, being so long unlived in. Peter analysed the emotion he was feeling, with tired detachment. It was not fear . . . It was horror. He must go – he must go. He must keep moving. *Move – don't think,* he told himself.

'What's up?'

'I'm off.'

'Oh. Why?'

'If you didn't ask so many questions you might get more answers.'

Peter walked into the hallway with one level of his awareness congratulating him on his ready wit, and the other deeper levels in restless movement about the consuming knot of worry in his stomach.

Professor Stanton was coming out of his study with a coffee mug in his hand.

'You off, are you, Peter?'

Mr Stanton's voice reverberated in the hallway – or, more probably, only in Peter's head. 'Yes.' He was so wound up, the word shot out as a hiss. he was moving fast now, almost in flight again as he tore open the front door and slammed it behind him in one movement.

Professor Stanton carried the empty coffee mug into the front room where Isobel was sitting staring down at the sandwiches in the manner of a fortune teller who could draw dark secrets from their random disposition. Her father saw she was upset.

'Lovers' tiff?' he enquired lightly.

'Not you, too.'

'I only wondered. Peter just went out as though the hounds of hell were after him.'

'He's a funny boy,' said Isobel casually, adopting an adult phrase yet continuing to read the riddle of the sandwich plate.

'Funny's one word for it.' Mr Stanton sat down

beside his daughter and put his arm around her. He felt her stiffen, but having made the gesture could not retract it without appearing equally cold or so sensitive to her mood that she would somehow gain an advantage over him. He kept the initiative by squeezing her shoulder reassuringly. How should he begin . . .?

'What's up at school?'

'Nothing much.'

'Do you get on with everyone?' No answer. 'I suppose they're all just ordinary, modern boys and girls.' 'Modern' struck the right note, he felt.

'Yes. I suppose so. Actually I don't talk to them much.'

'Except for Peter.'

'Yes, if you like.'

'And he's just another fella, is he?' The joke fell flat.

Silence. The Professor started to shuffle out some platitudes.

'I feel sorry sometimes for young people today. They have problems to deal with which we never had to consider. Like how to spend all that money they seem to have! It's not surprising some of them go wrong, somewhere along the line – some of us did, too, of course. Well – obviously. But mums and dads can't help worrying, though. About things like drugs and – oh – glue sniffing . . . things like tht. Everyone's so sophisticated these days, aren't they? These dismal days. Or cynical – that's a better word, probably. But perhaps it's not the same in the country – what do you think?'

'How do I know?'

'Because – ' He lost patience. 'Bella, I'm asking you if there's any silliness going on at school. People taking drugs – drinking. That sort of thing.'

'Don't look at me.' Isobel was sullen and uninterested.

'I didn't suggest . . . Isobel, can you look at me when I'm talking to you?' He dropped his arm from her shoulder. 'How am I to talk to you as a grown-up, if you never make the least attempt to behave like one?' Even as he spoke he knew this was the wrong approach.

Isobel gave him a challenging stare. 'Just talk to me however you want to.'

'Fair enough. Has Peter got in with a bad lot? Is he taking something, do you know?'

She was shocked into a straight response. 'No – I'm sure he isn't.'

The Professor put his arm back round her shoulder, lovingly, as he thought. 'How can you be – how would you have any way of telling?'

'Where did you get that idea from?'

'From him – looking at him – being with him. There's something wrong with him, Isobel. Something fundamentally *wrong*. It could be drugs – it could be he's just unstable, or—'

'He's the most sensible person I've ever met! And the kindest!' At that moment it didn't matter whether it was true or not; Peter's need for defence overflowed the narrow banks of truth. 'Do you know what you are, Dad?'

'You tell me, then!' He hated 'Dad' rather than 'Daddy'. Suddenly they were both furious.

'You're a one-parent family!'

*'What?'*

'You're clinging and possessive and you try to protect me from life in all the wrong ways! Let go!' She tore herself from his imprisoning arm and bumped into the coffee table before striding to the window. His voice pursued her, stridently.

'And just where did you read all that nonsense?'
'Ah, but it's true, isn't it?'
'It's nonsense and you know it!'
She ignored this. 'Well, I don't need you. You think I need you – I don't. If you want to know I think you're selfish and I hate you!'
'Oh that old game!'
'It's not a game! When I finally get a friend – a proper friend I've picked myself – you can't take it, can you? You can't wait to get back to like we used to be when I was your lovely, stupid little girl and you were – you're jealous of Peter!'
'You've talked enough rubbish – now it's *my* turn!'
'To talk rubbish? That's about it! I'm telling you, I choose my own friends! Don't you start on me!'
Mr Stanton let silence back into the room. Anything was preferable to this screaming match. It seemed this was the regular pattern of their lives these days: bitter arguments interspersed with mute, untrusting truces. He leant back and rubbed his head, unconscious of the action. Isobel took this to signal his surrender. Her chest was heaving with fury.
Mr Stanton got up and went to the mantelpiece, keeping his back to her. He spoke softly, bewildered.
'How did we start all this? What's it about, for God's sake? I only want what's best for you. In your heart of hearts you *know* that, Bella. Peter Ford . . .' Perhaps he was too tired to go on.
Isobel answered him equally quietly. 'Peter's my best friend. That's all. He doesn't take drugs. Nothing like that. All right, sometimes he's unhappy. Well – who's happy? Who's happy all the time?'
Then she left the room in an emotional rush, slamming the door. Her father found himself growing more and more angry with the self-pity he perceived

in her. In his head, Professor Stanton began to go through all the swearwords he had ever used or heard.

Blankness. Peter found the events and stresses of the last weeks had bred in him the ability to unfocus his thoughts and let his brain float free in his skull. It was a dangerous gift when you were riding a bicycle. He went straight over a road junction, looking neither left nor right.

He was going home by a route that led him nowhere near Culver Wood. It was too unfamiliar a way on which to use auto-pilot. Where was he now? He'd missed a turning. He didn't recognize the farm buildings in the distance at first. It gave him a sharp jolt – even here, in the surroundings he'd known for a lifetime, he was more of a stranger than when . . . It didn't bear thinking on. Just live day to day. Moment to moment. Let come what might come. The trick remained to keep one's sanity intact. And to do that, it was essential to ignore the inexplicable. He rode on, consciously unfurrowing his brow, calming his exterior in the hope that some kind of peace would work its way inwards. When you tried to define it, what was reality, anyway? That's if you cared to think about it at all – which Peter did not. Not at the moment.

Home. Here was a constant reality. Every corner of the house held a hundred incidents of his past, so thoroughly intermingled as to lose their separate identity and become one complex, indestructible part of his experience and personality.

His father had been watching television in the front room, taking a lukewarm interest in the day's news, while his mother was in the kitchen taking no interest whatsoever in the preparation of the evening meal. As usual Peter had come in through the kitchen.

'Hi, Mum.'

'Hi.'

'Hi, Dad.'

'Hi.'

His return had been established with no blemish on the reigning household boredom.

Peter was now in the bathroom, looking at himself in the mirror. He did this from time to time, a keen student of his own physical development; though this evening the examination was of more interest to him than on other occasions. The mirror registered 'no change'. His face was still uncompromisingly smooth and guileless, rounded like a pebble instead of bearing the flinty facets he admired on the stern looks of certain sportsmen or film stars. But on close inspection, the face was, if not rugged, then at least marked by the events of the day. There were violet stains on the thick skin under his eyes and the eyes themselves were wider than usual and stared at him in a disconcerting fashion, transfixed by their own image. He could not read their expression as he flicked his gaze from one eye to the other. He was looking at himself so intently that the black pupils of his eyes became his points of attention, drawing him into their featureless darkness like camera lenses waiting for a shutter to be triggered.

The mirror shattered.

More exactly, it broke into two pieces with a splitting sound and one triangular piece fell into the basin and destroyed itself further. Peter could still see one eye in the remaining portion of mirror, but half his head was missing now, replaced by an area of plywood. The single eye had not lost its wide stare.

'What's happened?'

'Peter – what are you doing up there?'

'Are you all right?'

His mother had scuttled up the stairs like a panicked ewe. 'Are you all right?'

'Yeah. I'm OK. The mirror broke.'

By now his father had followed Mrs Ford into the little bathroom. 'The mirror broke? What do you mean?'

'It broke . . . I was just in here and it just broke. I didn't do anything.'

'You must have done something.' It was important to Mr Ford that the inconvenience caused should be attributable.

'I didn't – really I didn't. I was just in here and – I saw it go. It just happened.'

His father looked around the bathroom, giving the impression he was looking for some damning evidence, like a hammer. 'Well. That's a new one on me.' There was no likely implement in sight and not a mark on Peter.

'Oh Peter!' Mrs Ford was solemn. 'Seven years' bad luck, that is.'

'I told you – *I* didn't do it.'

'Well, it still counts, I should think.'

'Don't talk stupid.' His father's need to express anger turned on Mrs Ford. 'These things happen. There's always an explanation, if you think about it. Probably it was a change of temperature of some sort. See – the glass can expand and shrink in different degrees of temperature. In the desert you get these rocks that fire off chips from themselves because of the big changes in the temperature between day and night – it was on the telly. All you need is a basic flaw in the mirror and . . . You two get on downstairs. Give

Peter a cup of tea, love. Must have been a nasty shock. I'll deal with this.'

'Seven years' bad luck?' Peter looked less than lovingly at his mother's back as she preceded him down the stairs. For once his father had reacted more helpfully than his mother.

'Well, you know the old superstition. I don't *believe* it. It's just what people say.'

She went on, while Peter stopped half way down the stairs. He was shaking again. He gave no credence to his father's temperature theory because, even as the mirror shattered, he had been aware of a force within himself, a level of energy he had never felt before. By staring so intently into the mirror he had quite unconsciously brought this unknown force to bear. The same force that made him see phantom aeroplanes and enter the body of someone from the past? It seemed almost unimportant whether there was a connection or not. If you looked on these bizarre experiences as the symptoms of an illness, it was getting worse.

'I'm fine. Great, thanks.' The words echoed in the aisle of the village church and wafted up on the grey air to lodge in the wooden arches of the roof. Peter went on more quietly, 'How are you, Mr Holroyd?'

'Oh, not too bad, you know, Peter.'

Mr Holroyd was in his shirtsleeves, polishing the brass eagle on the lectern stand, thereby confirming a rumour even Peter had heard. It was said that the two elderly sisters employed to clean the church were 'past it' and that Mr Holroyd 'went round' after they departed. Peter was disappointed to see the vicar was not wearing an apron: that at least was optimistic exaggeration. The great black bible lay on the stone flags beside a plastic dustpan and brush. Perhaps Mr Holroyd 'went round' the graveyard, too, with nail scissors, to improve on the verger's work with the push mower. Peter's father had recently tried to sell the vicar a motor mower . . .

'What do you want, Peter?' Mr Holroyd stopped burnishing the eagle, irritated by the boy standing watching him in silence.

'What?'

'Or did you come in here just to get away from some game or other?'

'No – there's no game.' That was the case exactly: Peter was here with serious purpose. Two days had passed without incident and in the long night hours he had lost sleep over a crucial dilemma. To tell or not to tell? His decision, arrived at with a relief that of itself justified the choice, had been to put off telling anyone anything until he had at least taken all the practical steps he himself could to clarify his predicament.

There were certain strands to investigate, starting here . . .

'No – I'm just here by myself. To see you.'

'Well, I'm glad we've got that straight. It's just you and me, then, so get on with it. I've a lot to do.'

'Yes, I can see.'

The vicar suppressed with difficulty his growing ill-humour. 'What is it, Peter?'

'Oh yeah, well . . . we're doing the wars of Napoleon in history and we've each got to give ourselves a project to do. Something on local history of the times – you know?'

Mr Holroyd's face lit up. An East Anglian by birth, he had adopted Kent with the fervour of a religious convert. In the twelve years of his tenure here he had gained more knowledge about this area, past and present, than even his oldest parishioners could lay claim to. Happily, the locals were able to denigrate his wisdom as 'book-learnt' and thus of poorer quality than the hand-woven tales they could themselves tell, if they could bring them to mind.

'I see! Interesting. I could bore you for hours on that. Or did you have something specific already in mind?'

Mr Holroyd was making it easy. 'Um, yes – sort of. I thought I might do something about an individual – just one man – make a picture of his life and what it was like – the kind of views he had and so on.'

'Aha, aha . . .' Mr Holroyd nodded encouragingly.

'There was a mill near Ruckinge – the man had a good name for a story. Deft.'

'Perfect – this is perfect. Where on earth did you get him from – Deft?'

'I don't know really. Probably local stories, handed down. I don't really remember.' He dashed on, 'I thought I'd concentrate on a period around the year 1803.'

'I'd dearly like to know how these stories do get about . . . But, *Deft* – this is splendid. Come on, then, into the sacristy.'

Mr Holroyd bustled off in a tangle of limbs, highly enthusiastic.

The sacristy was warm in the evening light. In some puritan way the warmth seemed at odds with a place of religion. They sat in the dark oak window seat that overlooked the graveyard.

'Well now, how best can I help you? You can learn quite a lot about Deft – that would be the father in

1803 – yes – from *Rural Kent Under the Georges*. I'll lend you my copy – on condition you turn the pages with great care. Oh no – I lent it out the other week – but I'll certainly let you have a look when I get it back. *If* I get it back. What do they say? "Neither a borrower nor a –" '

'He was a famous figure then, was he – Deft?'

'Well, hardly that. But in local terms he was, perhaps. The elder Deft would be more an *infamous* figure, actually, to our modern eyes.'

'Yes?'

'Mmm. He made huge profits from the wars, you know – and thereafter, too. A very unpopular man, one senses. His son was a much better chap.'

'But I suppose his workers would be loyal to him?'

'What? Oh . . . I dare say there were those who put up with the old devil. But he did exploit them terribly, even for those unenlightened times. And he was a notorious miser, to add to his other faults. He ran through three wives, too. They all predeceased him. One has to imagine he gave them a pretty bad time. And then there was the case of young Swan . . .'

To Peter the slight pause expanded into an eternity of waiting. Mr Holroyd was thinking, smiling.

'Oh yes. They nearly had him there. This young lad, Jeremiah Swan – he worked for him, you see – Deft – but he hated it so much he took to running away. Now in those days that would have been against the law – no unions, then – but even so, he hardly deserved his eventual fate.'

'His fate?'

'He was taken by the fencibles – was it? – the second time, as I recall. It's actually in that book of mine somewhere – and on that same night he wound up dead in Deft's mill. Crushed in the machinery.'

The sense of the words hit Peter with a delayed action effect, so that for the next few seconds he was struggling to keep up with the vicar's onrushing chat.

'I say "machinery" – I mean, of course, the stone wheels that, um, grind the corn. You know the sort of thing? Massive great blocks of rounded stone, weighing a couple of tons each, I should think – if not more. You know the sort of thing?'

He was earnest and brilliantly cheerful. It wasn't right, Peter thought, that a vicar should relish the story in this way. But it was history, long dead. Like Jem Swan. He cleared his throat.

'Yes.'

'Well, now. He had one friend, did young Swan. A farm-worker from – I forget where, but somewhere near here, anyway – and he refused to believe old Deft's story about accidental death. Do you know, that ignorant farm-hand enlisted local support and tried to get Deft prosecuted? Extraordinary. He didn't get anywhere, as it turned out. Naturally not. The landowners of the district ganged up and supported Deft, and then the man didn't stand an earthly. But he had an effect, all the same. Deft had to mend his ways, his peers told him – and he did. His workers must still have hated him, one would guess, but the kind of ill-treatment he'd been handing out as a matter of course came to an end. What was that man's name . . . the farm-worker. Now he's the chap you want to do your project on! Quite a hero, in his way. Tom Garrett. That was it. Yes . . .'

Tom Garrett. Suddenly it seemed to Peter a terrible shame that there was in actuality no school project. Tom Garrett deserved attention. And had Peter really seen the man – and mistrusted him? Tom had stood to the last by his friend, Jem . . .

Peter.

– Jem.

'What happened to Tom Garrett?'

'I don't know. I don't know everything, you know!' Mr Holroyd laughed. 'No – you stick to Deft. There'll have been plenty written about him, if you care to ferret it out.'

Peter stood up and put on a frown. 'Oh, I don't know. I might do something else for the project. Something easier.'

Mr Holroyd was disappointed. 'Oh.'

'Yes – we don't have much time and . . .'

'Oh, well, do as you like, of course . . .'

'I'm sorry, Mr Holroyd. It was really interesting, anyway.' He searched for a word that would please. 'Fascinating.'

'Well, yes – *I* think so.' Mr Holroyd was still huffy, so Peter tried again.

'*Really* fascinating. Thanks.'

*And so easy.* Peter had been optimistic that the vicar might have some small knowledge of Deft, as an erstwhile power in the district, but if My Holroyd could not only chatter on about the miller but also about Tom Garrett and 'young Swan' and had an old book where it was all laid out in print, then . . .

He saw that his approach had been flawed from the start. On the one hand, if only he knew what had happened on that night in 1803, then clearly there was no way in which he could substantiate it. And if others knew about it, then it was conceivable he could have picked up the knowledge unconsciously somewhere and brought the scene to life in his imagination.

Except he hadn't, of course. His memory was that of actuality, not dreams. And had he stayed on as Jem Swan, he would have been mashed to death in the mill.

Peter remembered how the tree trunk had scraped his knee; how it had hurt.

# Nine

On Sunday Peter stood in another churchyard.

In its day the tombstone would have been a cut-price affair. Now it was even less impressive; a low slab that had been gnawed at by the elements, barely visible in thick grass under a hedge. The inscription would not last another century.

Jer i h Swa 1789-1803

Perhaps Tom Garrett had arranged for the burial to have at least this degree of substance. Peter felt . . . only surprise that he felt so little. Jem Swan was a complete stranger at this remove of time and he experienced no more than a vague disgust at the ghastly death and a vague pity about one so long forgotten.

It had taken all his free time over the last days, establishing that he and Jem Swan could not possibly be related by blood, and tracking down his grave. Peter had done miles on the bike, cycling from church to church to examine parish records.

The early service had finished and the worshippers were leaving the church, taking their time about it, as though to make their numbers seem greater. A middle-aged couple walking arm in arm stared at him in his lonely corner of the graveyard.

It was a conundrum. He had shared a part of

Swan's life, but could feel little for him. If that was all he had learnt, then he had wasted time he could perhaps have spent more profitably in Culver Wood, or searching for the stranger who shared his interest in the wood and who had possibly been an onlooker at the taking of Swan – or had an ancestor who had. Thinking about it, Peter was positive he should not seek out the stranger. It was instinct at its most persuasive and he welcomed it; promising himself instead that he would look in Culver Wood again, as soon as possible.

He wondered what Isobel was thinking about him. He had barely said a word to her for days. He turned away from Swan's grave and left the churchyard without a backward glance. She had looked miserable. No doubt she'd come running back if he was nice to her.

It was another brilliant morning. The road and verges still gleamed with moisture, so that every bobble of asphalt or blade of grass was outlined distinctly in reflected light from the sun.

Isobel was strung tight with dislike.

'Leave me alone, will you? You're more trouble than you're worth.'

'Probably.'

He had the front wheel of his bike in front of hers, keeping her trapped in tight against the kerb, preventing her from travelling the last hundred metres to the school.

'My father thinks you're a drug addict, by the way.'

'Does he?' Peter was amazed.

'And I defended you. Again. I must be mad. You're not worth it. Probably you do sniff glue, anyway.'

'No, I don't. I'm sorry I haven't been very friendly

just lately.' It wasn't easy to say and opened the way for Isobel.

'Friendly? Friendly? You do speak English, don't you? You know what friendly means? Well, I was your friend, but I'm not now and you know why?'

'Because I haven't been friendly, I suppose.'

'You're dead right there.'

'Well, now I am friendly.'

'And that's it, is it? Thank you very much for noticing me at all.'

Time for the big lie. 'Well, I was . . . thinking about you.'

'No, you weren't. Don't give me that. Were you?'

'Yup. I was. I have been for days.' Surely that sounded soft enough.

'Well it didn't show.'

'Well, it wouldn't. I mean . . . But I was thinking about you.'

'What were you thinking, then?'

She had already shown him a good angle on this one. He sighed. 'I don't know. I got this feeling that, well . . . your father doesn't approve of me.'

'Well, you're right there.'

'But it's more than that. He doesn't think I'm – um – he doesn't think I'm the right sort of friend for you.'

More thoughtfully: 'Doesn't he?'

'Well, I got the feeling he'd rather we weren't friendly. He's a good bloke, your dad. And when you look at it from his point of view – well – he's got a point.'

'That's silly.'

'No, it isn't. I'm nothing special, am I? I don't want to be, if it comes to that. Your father, well, he's like any dad – he wants the best for you. Look at it any way you like . . . that's not me.'

'Oh.'

'If you really like someone – ' Oh, this was hard – 'you do want the best for them. You don't want to bring them down. That's what I've been thinking about. About you and me. And I do like you.'

Funny. You said something and it took on life and truth, even when you thought you were only fooling around. Yes, he liked her a lot. He found himself going red. 'I do. I like you, but I'm – me. I'm just . . . sort of dull.' He ploughed on to the resolution of his ploy, not feeling proud of himself. 'You'd be making a big mistake, hanging around with me. I think your father's right.' Then he added recklessly, 'About most things, probably.' This last phrase brought him back to a complete, satisfactory untruth.

'Yes – well – he's not. You're not a drug addict. Can I go on now?'

Her body had relaxed. The wild pony had been gentled, though at a heavy cost to Peter's self esteem. He backed up his bike and was nearly hit by Patel as he raced up the road. Patel rang his bell but did not look back.

Peter answered Isobel. 'Yeah. You can go on. Sorry.'

'And stop apologizing for yourself.'

Better and better. It had been worth it. He'd have to be careful, though.

'Here – Pete!'

A boy from his class had ballooned a shot in Peter's direction. He let the dented rubber ball run up from his toe to his thigh, then bounced the ball on his knee before allowing it to fall on to his other foot, which struck the ball back with pin-point accuracy.

It was lunchtime and Isobel was by his side at the

mesh fence surrounding the baking hot recreation area.

'Oh – superb,' the boy called mockingly. 'Have you seen the board yet? You need all the practice you can get!' He took a throw-in from an arbitrary point near the buckled metal five-a-side goal. Patel was goalie and protested vigorously. He didn't once glance in Peter's direction.

Peter was sorry his friendship with Isobel had the effect of losing him his other friends. She was unreceptive to teachers and lessons and positively discouraged people from liking her. She was determined to be an outsider and now Peter was one too. Though perhaps it was the other way around – she was drawn to Peter because he was even more of an outsider than she.

'What was that about?' Isobel was anxious he shouldn't withdraw into his shell again.

'Don't you look at the board?'

'No.'

'I'm in the team on Saturday.'

'Oh. Well done.'

She meant it. Isobel was entirely on his side. It was a selfish reason for which to like her – because she liked him and he was sorry for her. And yet, and yet . . . there was more to it than that. For instance, he wouldn't dream of confiding in Patel or the others. That was another thing in her favour. Perhaps one of a multitude of reasons to like her. You could talk to her.

'D'you ever have nightmares?'

'Not any more. Not real ones. Just worry dreams – losing things, getting lost. You know.'

'Yeah. I had a weird dream a couple of nights ago.' For some reason all girls were interested in dreams, he remembered.

'What about?'

'It was like I was someone else – in another time. In history.'

'You'd seen a film or something – right?'

'No. I was this person in history and he was me. It was weird, because I went where he wanted to go – said what he wanted to say. I didn't have any choice. But it was incredibly real. Not very nice, really. I couldn't do anything. It was like being trapped in a stranger but he was you.'

'You couldn't do what you wanted to do?'

'Yeah.'

'That always happens in dreams. You've got to get away from something but your legs won't work. That's always happening in dreams.'

He was annoyed. 'It wasn't like that.'

'Or you're going into a room and you know it's going to be terrible when you get in but you go in all the same.'

'It wasn't like that.' This was hopeless.

'I had a crazy dream once. I can remember it really well. There was this circus – only it wasn't a circus – it could have been a zoo – and you could order a meal there . . .'

She rambled on about her boring dream. Peter didn't listen properly, but he didn't interrupt either. He guessed it would take a few days before their relationship was fully re-established. He wouldn't mention the wood; not yet.

One had to admit Professor Stanton was a polished performer. In some strange way the Ministry of Defence land was unrecognizable on the television screen, though Peter once caught a glimpse of Mrs Robertson's house, over the Professor's shoulder.

It was windy. Obviously the programme had been made some days ago. Mr Stanton talked to a local television reporter, referring to objects laid out on a long table in front of them. Behind, the whole site looked a quiet hive of organized activity, with lines and trenches strictly demarcated. Peter had a notion that the archaeologists, assisted by several casual workers, had been asked to bunch in together in order to provide an interesting background.

'Not only do we hope to come across more from this grave,' the Professor was saying, 'but we're still hopeful there'll be further graves in the vicinity.'

'Perhaps we could take a look at some more of your, er . . .' The reporter was in a hurry, but he didn't fluster Mr Stanton.

'Well, surely. Here, for example.' The camera moved in on Mr Stanton's pointing finger. 'A shield boss, layered over with silver gilt. You can see there's some kind of animal dancing on it, and that around the rim –' He turned the conical object – 'is some exceptionally fine silverwork. We're looking at an officer, in all probability – and quite an important one at that.'

'A general, you think?'

'Oh, doubtful. The whole theme of this grave is Frankish. The man might well have been captured by the Roman legions and allowed his freedom on condition he served in the Roman army. That wasn't uncommon at the end of Roman rule. And, as the coin showed us, this would have been very shortly before the Romans set sail back to what was left of their glory.'

Peter's father shifted in his chair. 'You could have helped there, couldn't you – at the dig.'

'Mmm.'

'Could have been on the telly.' Mr Ford was regretful.

Meanwhile a shot of Stutfall Castle came up. The gapped and crumbling, vaguely pentagonal walls were perched halfway down the old sea cliff below Lympne. The Professor was still talking.

'In Roman days the fort was called Portus Lemanis. Possibly the headquarters of the Roman fleet for a time. There were troops from Tournai stationed there. Perhaps our man would have served there himself. A man of some authority, as I said, as witness the several finger and arm rings – all made of gold.' The camera was showing the table again.

'Amazing,' said Mr Ford. 'Probably means a lot more to you than me, though, with you being good at history.'

'History's a bore,' said Peter.

The Professor continued in languid tones over a shot of a particularly deep trench in which Angus was on his hands and knees, working – or pretending to work – with a penknife.

'A North-South grave. By this time, at the start of the fifth century, Christianity was coming to the fore. But our man was of older beliefs – no West-East grave for *him*.'

'That's how the Christians were buried?' the reporter queried dutifully.

'That's right. And if you see these . . .' Again the camera obeyed the Professor . . . 'we're definitely looking at what one might call "pagan artwork" on these three buckles. All have animal ornamentation and are chip-carved. There are several such graves on the continent, and one now feels fairly sure this is indeed a *laeti* grave – the grave of a Frankish convert to the Roman cause. Now that's exciting, because such graves are exceptionally rare in this country.'

'Even in Kent?' The reporter was joking and both men could now be seen smiling at one another.

'Even in Kent.'

The reporter instantly became serious again. 'Leaving aside monetary value, what article interests you most?'

'Personally? Well, I'm very attached to his knife, here – it's in such good condition. The bone handle is partially intact and the silver inlay is – well, see for yourself.'

The camera closed in on the knife in the Professor's hands.

'Amazing . . .' Mr Ford yawned.

'Yes – that's what I think.' Peter got up and wandered into the kitchen, where his mother was unblocking the plug-hole in the sink. She ruffled his hair, leaving wet carrot peelings in it, then plunged her hands back into the water. He went out to the garden, brushing his fingers through his hair.

Almost seven thirty, the kitchen clock had said. He'd get to bed early tonight. It was the day of the match tomorrow.

'Don't you want to come tomorrow?'

'I've got better things to do with my Saturdays.'

'Such as?' Isobel had hoped to go in the Range Rover.

'Such as: work. Did you enjoy the programme?'

They were still sitting in front of the now blank television screen.

'Not really.'

'I'll tell you a secret. Nor did I.'

Isobel was intrigued. 'Why not?'

'Well, when we discussed the idea, the general thought was that we'd be dealing with a big excavation. We'd be able to show someone finding something; everyone working hard all over the field – starting work on new graves and so on. The whole thing should have been on a much grander scale.'

Isobel relented. 'Actually I did quite like the programme. You were jolly good. You know – you kept it simple.

The Professor grimaced wryly. 'Yes, it's a great talent, isn't it? Well it wasn't hard to do, because what you saw there was all we had to show.' He shifted his weight and leant forward, looking at the grey television screen. 'All we've had for days.

'Oh. I didn't get that.'

'You see, I'm beginning to think there aren't any more graves. Somehow it's a one-off. It's just a feeling I have. The trouble is, we'll have to prove that and it'll take weeks. Your Peter . . .' He shook his head, then asked in a neutral tone, 'How is he?'

'He's all right. He's playing tomorrow – that's why I'm going.'

'Ah.' Mr Stanton pursed his lips, demonstrating that he was thinking of adding to the syllable, but apparently nothing worth saying occurred to him.

After a while Isobel said she thought she would go and run her bath.

That night Peter was woken by a noise he could not at first identify. He was grateful to be awake; his dream had been unpleasant.

In it, he and Mr Holroyd were seated at a table on the stage of the assembly hall at school and Mr Holroyd was addressing the entire school, telling them how he had discovered a stranger in their midst.

'I don't say Peter Ford is evil – that is not for me to judge. What I do say is that he cannot be trusted to behave like a normal human being. Perhaps you will be so good as to tell us why, Peter.' In the dream Peter had stood up, embarrassed, saying he didn't know – he honestly didn't know – it wasn't his fault . . .

Now he struggled for a grip on the real world. Something had woken him. There it was again, a sharp rap on the window. He threw back the duvet and waited for confirmation of his suspicion. Yes – another tap, heavier this time. Someone was throwing fragments of gravel at the window – someone called Isobel Stanton, for sure. Though why? He turned his bedside light on and stumbled to the curtains, drew them and pulled up the open window still higher, so that he could put his head out.

'What is it?'

Isobel stepped out of the shadows into the square of light cast from Peter's room: only it was not Isobel, it was the man from Culver Wood.

Peter's head jerked back by reflex and he banged his head on the window frame. The man put out a hand.

'Stay where you are. Don't be frightened.'

In the gloom it was impossible to see those distinctive, unfathomable eyes. Peter was frozen, his fingers gripping the windowsill.

'Do you . . . know who I am?' The stranger whispered.

'No.' His voice refused to function properly.

'Ah . . .' The man was disappointed, Peter thought. 'I'm . . . your friend. You must believe that. I'm not going to harm you, I just . . . want you to listen to me.'

'Go away.'

'Do you know what a risk I've taken in coming here?'

'I'm going to get my parents.'

'No.' There was authority in the man's voice. 'You won't. You want to hear what I have to say. It's this: that night in the wood I sent a message – a signal. I've had the answer now.'

'Please go away.'

The man's speech had become more sure, as if he had only needed to get back into practice. 'That's what I came to tell you. I am going away. We both are. I've broken the rules, I know, coming here. But we both of us know it's gone wrong. The task is ended. We've been here too long and it went wrong.'

Peter said desperately, 'I hear what you're saying, but I don't know what you mean!'

The man took a cautious step nearer. 'That doesn't matter.' Peter could now see his eyes, boring into his own. 'You've been having some strange times, young man, I shouldn't wonder.'

'Yes.'

'Well . . . not much longer now. It's over.'

Peter heard his father coughing in the next room. He looked nervously towards the sound, and when he looked back the man was no longer visible. He heard the quiet voice again, though.

'It's over. You understand: it's over.'

Peter saw a vague shape moving round to the front of the house. He heard the latch on the gate and a moment later the gate was closed.

He was drained and dizzy. He wandered away from the window and it was as though he had been given an injection of some kind, for he collapsed on to the bed and into a deep, untroubled sleep.

The next morning he felt unexpectedly relaxed, as if a fever had broken. As he packed his football gear he was actively looking forward to the big match.

It was an unsatisfactory explanation, but he told himself he was relieved because the madman from Culver Wood was going away for good – that much at least seemed certain.

'Push out! Push out!'

The match had been going for about half an hour and the sportsmaster was already hoarse. They were under attack again, Isobel saw. The opposing team didn't seem markedly better to her eyes, if you made the exception of a surprisingly tubby winger who had the speed and ability to cause considerable alarm every time he got the ball and who had already scored once. But, all in all, it really wasn't much of a game, Isobel thought.

Hovering near the opposite touchline to Isobel and the bulk of the spectators, Peter was frustrated. This was the pitch on which he'd played out of his skin to win his place on the team, yet today he was far from being an outstanding player. It was impossible to show that he too was fast and skilful when he had barely had a kick. As a newcomer to the team he had largely been ignored by the others on his side. He was sure things would be very different if he was given the ball as often as his opposite number, the heavy-weight winger Peter had inwardly designated 'Fatty', although he looked rather more solid than flabby.

The sportsmaster was standing next to the teacher in charge of the other side. 'Your lad's a real prospect, John,' he said in a cracked voice, already conditioning himself to the prospect of defeat.

His old friend and rival agreed, while keeping his eyes on the game. 'I'll tell you, Terry, before that boy's left us, we'll have nothing left to win.'

'The game's not over yet,' Terry said without conviction.

'No?'

Fatty picked this moment to score his second goal with a humming long-range drive which was still lifting as it rattled into the netting. The referee's whistle chirruped and he pointed dramatically to the centre circle.

'No?' John asked again, politely.

Peter's team-mates were manifestly dispirited as they organized themselves for the re-start. Waiting for the whistle, Peter jumped up and down on the spot, trying to work up some determination. Just let him have one shot at goal – just one . . .

In the event, it seemed that it was Fatty who would again have the opportunity that Peter longed for. When the game began once more he intercepted a pass and raced away down the wing with the ball at his feet. Peter began to run back to a point where he might confront the goalscorer, already judging that he was likely to be the last line of defence.

'Peter! Take him, Peter!'

In a curious way the captain of his team was offering his acceptance and friendship by this frantic shout. The spectators were shouting, too.

Peter's rapid, instinctive calculation was proved correct when Fatty tore past a despairing defender and cut infield. Peter sprinted towards him at an angle, attempting to force him wide again, and for a second or two both players were side by side, moving just about flat out, until Peter found the extra inch of pace to put himself marginally in front. He feinted to commit himself to a tackle and Fatty was fooled and immediately swerved for his final lunge in towards the penalty area.

With a fraction of a second left it was a question of timing the real tackle to perfection and –

*Snap*.

His eyes were closed and the warm sun shone pink and gold through his eyelids. He was lying down. The sounds of the football match had vanished.

A voice spoke teasingly.

# Ten

'Open your eyes . . .'

It was a light voice; a girl's voice, with careful, tight vowel sounds. An upper class voice.

Peter breathed in the warm, dusty smell of the field into which his back was pressed. A field of grain of some sort. It was so hot he had no wish at all to open his eyes. He wasn't afraid. It would be pleasant to drift off to sleep, lying here with his hands behind his head.

'Open wide . . .'

His eyes opened and were struck by a sheet of white light. The girl laughed. He was temporarily blinded. Muscles moved in his body and he sat up and spoke, again feeling the strange sensation of his voice box vibrating independently of his control.

'You daft idiot.'

'You're lazy.'

The immediate blackness that had replaced the light was in turn superseded by dancing motes of red and green. His sight adjusted itself. He was looking at a girl who knelt beside him in a loose grey dress. Stray heads of wheat lay here and there in the rutted field, but harvest time had come and gone, for all around them the golden, woody stalks of wheat had been cropped short. The girl's hair was the colour of the wheat and her eyes were a pale, diluted blue, lively with amusement.

'That's dangerous, that,' Peter was saying. She held a small square of mirror in her hand.

'At least it woke you up.'

'I wasn't asleep.'

'Will I see you tonight?'

'If you like.'

'Usual time.'

'Usual place. Yes.'

'I'll bring some food.'

'Good-oh.' That didn't sound like him. He'd never said 'good-oh' in his life. 'I'll bring some ginger beer,' he was saying.

'All right.' She asked politely, 'Are you going to lie here all day?'

'I might. I'm tired.'

'Aren't we all? It's all this waiting every day. Will they come tonight, do you think?'

She got up. Her legs were thin under the shapeless dress. Then, completely sure of herself, she just walked away from him to a warped old gate some distance away.

Peter found he was getting to his feet. They were on the edge of the field; beyond the gate a dirt road carried a central scalp of grass. The girl climbed the gate with ease and dropped down on to the dirt track. She looked back then, head cocked to one side, teasingly, and gave a little wave. She walked away.

Peter wanted to look around him, but instead he was slumping back down on to the knobbly, impacted earth, careless of the sharp bristles of the wheat stalks. Going down, he saw he wore torn black trousers and plimsolls. The trousers were too big for him and a belt was drawn tight on his waist. Curiously, he was at peace with himself, unwilling to think. It was a seductively hot summer's day. Whoever, whatever he was, he was comfortable out here in the hot, heavy air, feeling the sun working its way into his skin.

Once he thought about the football match. It seemed light years away.

Once a Common Blue butterfly flew by haphazardly. It was the same colour as the girl's eyes.

Time was a solid, indivisible block, composed not of seconds and minutes, but of a single weighty silence that might either be compressing the hours or expanding them.

Perhaps Peter fell asleep. He was aware his eyes had closed again, were held shut by the pressure of the sun. A thrush started to sing and the idea came to him that it was only through sounds and the intervals between them that one could actually measure time.

Another sound registered itself. A droning noise, though not that of an insect.

Before he knew it Peter was rolling over and bouncing to his feet.

It was a Hurricane. The fighter plane was flying in over Peter, quite low in the sky. As it passed overhead he had his hand shading his eyes, looking up at its belly and the rigid spread of its wings. The droning sounds were louder and more indistinct, broken into the component parts that made the sum total of the noise. Peter remembered that Patel had once demonstrated the effectiveness of the waste disposal unit in the sink in the kitchen above his father's shop. He had put a plastic spoon down it and the machinery had had difficulty in chewing it up. The warplane above Peter made a similar, reluctant grinding noise.

As it flew away, growing smaller, the aeroplane settled even lower in the blue sky and a streamer of dark, fast-moving smoke erupted from the engine cowling, increasing by the second.

Peter began to charge after the plane through the rustling, breaking wheat stubble.

*Snap*.

Night and fire. He was reminded of the torchlight outside Tom Garrett's cottage. But this was an oily conflagration he was running towards; a swollen, churning mass of flame and smoke, both illuminating and obscuring a clump of trees in the middle of a meadow. A plane had crashed there: a bomber, by the size of it. There were stars in the clear night sky and he was running fast, thumping his feet down into the turf. He had a bottle in his hand and he pumped it backwards and forwards like a relay runner's baton, leaning so far forward in his efforts to move faster that he was close to falling.

Silhouetted against the black and golden havoc he saw a figure move jerkily from the trees and the huge crumpled shape which burned amongst them. Now flames danced through the dry leaves of the trees. Running still, he felt himself shouting, *'Fran! Fran!'*

For a second it seemed the girl gave a small, teasing wave, as she had at the gate to the field; then the stricken bomber exploded and she was enveloped in rolling fire and the dark bat shapes of flying debris. A second later Peter was blown backwards to the ground.

He was partially winded and when he had hauled himself up, he found he was moving more slowly. Nearer the great plane it was as bright as the day had been and ten times as hot. Rivulets of fire ran like liquid lava through the grass. He saw a burning, blistering section of fuselage. On it was imprinted a fat black cross outlined in white. It curled and burned.

The explosion must have picked her up and thrown her forwards many metres. She lay on her face, still in the grey dress. The bottle was no longer in Peter's hand. He reached down, sickened by the acrid smells gusting from the trees, grabbed the girl's lifeless hands and began to pull her away from the burning streams of petrol. She was completely relaxed and he thought she must be dead. She was heavy, too, and her back arched upwards at an unnatural angle as he tugged her along. A phrase came to Peter and lingered in his mind: *'She's broken.'*

He was pulling her ever farther away when a second explosion ripped through the air. The blast blew Peter's legs from under him and he fell awkwardly, letting go of the girl. His head hit something hard.

It was black. His eyes were shut again. His hair clung to his head like tar. He could hear voices just above him.

'You could barely see a mark on her.'

Someone was wiping his face.

'Funny, isn't it. He looks worse than she does, but he's still breathing normal. It's just a cut.'

'That's young Sadler.'

'Who?'

'Phil Sadler. Helps his mother on the farm. I wondered who it would be. Not many kids round here just now.'

'Trust Jerry to get kids.

*Let me guess your surname. Sadler.* The young girl, Fran – *Frances*, that was her name – would become Mrs Robertson, old and crippled and blind. He opened his eyes and was unsurprised to see the two men kneeling by him were dressed in the rough woollen uniforms of soldiers. One carried a shotgun;

it was the other who had been using his handkerchief to wipe Peter's face. A shotgun . . .?

'All right, are you?' said the man with the bloodied handkerchief. Beyond the soldiers, a hundred metres away, the German bomber was a crackling skeleton on its tall-standing funeral pyre, which cast shadows across the gaunt, seamed faces of the two soldiers, who must both have been well over fifty years old.

'Yes.' He sat up, feeling nauseous and dizzy. 'Where's Frances?'

The soldier tucked the stained handkerchief into his tunic pocket. 'They're putting her in the brigadier's car.'

The car was an ancient silver Rolls Royce, Peter saw. An elderly man in a tight-fitting uniform was getting into the driver's seat; two other men in civilian clothes, wearing armbands, stood on the running boards. The car's great staring headlights came on and swept round with the car, dazzling Peter for a moment. As the little mirror had . . .

Mrs Robertson's eyes had been a clear, joyful blue. Later it would be hard to tell what colour they had been and harder still to guess what she really thought deep under that carapace of age and the act she put on. 'Is she alive?' he was asking.

'Yes,' said the man with the shotgun. 'Let's be having you, young man.'

The two old soldiers helped Peter to his feet.

'Can you walk?' said Shotgun.

'Yes.'

The other man took Peter's arm. Peter looked over at the copse, where half a dozen soldiers were waiting for the fire to become less intense. The trees would become nothing but charred stems.

Shotgun said, 'I'll tell you what, boy, if you're

responsible for the girl being here, I wouldn't be in your shoes for anything. Not for all the tea in China.' His gnarled face was grotesque in the background of fire.

*Snap.*

He was in a violent collision: someone cried out in pain. People were shouting.

He had fallen beside Fatty, who was whimpering and writhing, clutching at his knee with little patting movements, as though the pain was so great that a continuous hold would add to the agony. Peter got up. The shouting seemed far away. Though he wasn't hurt he was unable to think clearly. By his side, the referee was bending over Fatty. Players from both sides had formed a ragged circle around them.

John, the opposition's team manager, came bustling up full of righteous fury.

'You animal – what do you think you're doing!'

'That's enough of that,' said the referee, then blew a blast on the whistle he had forgotten about. 'Right – you – straight off.' He pointed to the touchline.

Without another look at Fatty or anyone else, Peter walked in the direction indicated. The enraged John abandoned his badly injured player and trotted after Peter.

'Where do you spend your holidays, son? Eh? Eh? South America?' He was quite literally shaking with rage.

'It was an accident,' Peter said heavily.

'It was pure, mindless, calculated cynicism!' In his excitement, John bellowed random phrases from the sporting pages of the newspapers. 'You don't expect to see that kind of animal behaviour at schoolboy level!' Then even that area of his vocabulary deserted him and he fell back on a line which had struck him as effective, 'Where do you spend your holidays? South America?'

Peter stared at John and he shut his mouth with an audible snap. The boy's gaze was deadly cold. Peter said. 'Think of it like this. His head's already bigger than his stomach. I did him a favour.'

Terry arrived to intervene. 'Leave him be, John. He couldn't have meant to do it.'

'I'll tell you, Terry, he's never going to play again – I'll see to that! *And* we could bring a civil action!'

'Oh come on – that's plain silly.'

'Is it?'

'You're over-reacting, John, and you know it.' A sly note crept into Terry's reasonable tone. 'You wouldn't be jumping up and down quite so much if the kid had gone in on another player. Be honest.'

John was beside himself. 'Taking his side, are you?'

'Not at all, not at all. Oh no – he's got quite a talk coming to him, he has.'

'I'm sorry – that's not good enough!'

'We'll talk about it later, John – eh?'

John turned on his heel and returned to his injured star, and Terry and Peter went on towards the spectators.

'I don't know what to do about you, Ford.' Terry shook his head,but it was difficult to tell how cross he really was. 'If I were you, I'd get straight on home. We don't want to stir up tempers, do we? What got into you? I've never seen anything like it.' Peter didn't answer and Terry's voice hardened. 'Oh – fancy yourself a hard man, do you? Well, look out for trouble, then, because. . . .' Peter's stony stare silenced him as it had his friend.

Peter walked across to Isobel. Patel was hurrying over to join them. Everyone else ignored him.

Isobel was about to say something when Patel arrived, awestruck. 'I tell you, Peter, I've never seen anything like it. You nearly broke him in half. Talk about high – you really took him out.'

'I didn't mean to.'

'Tell that to the judge, eh? I wouldn't be in your shoes, I can tell you.'

*Not for all the tea in China.* 'Yeah. Well. See you around, Pat.'

'Oh, sure. Tough luck, Pete.'

Peter took Isobel's arm and led her away from the spectators, some of them disapproving parents. 'I didn't mean to, Isobel.' He was very tired again and hoped nothing odd was going to happen to him.

'That's not what it looked like.'

'I can't help that.'

She was kind. 'Shall I come with you? It's a long walk.' He smiled at her and she felt cross because she liked him smiling at her.

'Thanks. No. You stay here. You can tell me about the game tomorrow.'

'Are you coming over?'

He paused. 'Yes. Probably.'

His hair was wet from the shower as he cycled out of the all-but-deserted school. The caretaker had let him into the building in complete silence, as if by some bush telegraph system he had already heard the news of Peter's disgrace.

Peter's hair was even wetter some minutes later. Clouds had formed and burst with a rapidity that suggested spring had returned, refreshed, to do further battle before surrendering to summer. By now the match must be over. He didn't care. He was cycling home the long way and water ran down his neck and chilled it, although the afternoon was still warm.

It was lethargy rather than the rain that prompted him to seek shelter, however. On the main road there was a wooden bus shelter which in its time had seen a thousand personal dramas; a lonely outpost of lovers' quarrels and grim family silences; where the flattened beer cans of regular drinkers shared the floor with the tiny cigarette butts of schoolchildren who were learning the habit on a budget. As he wheeled his bicycle into the empty shelter he caught the sweet, doss-house smell that no amount of fresh air could quite dispel. He leant the bike against the grubby bench and stood inches away from the rain that dripped from the roof of the shelter.

What was one supposed to do? Get an interview with a psychiatrist? Ludicrous. Talk to Mr Holroyd? Worse still. Peter wouldn't consider telling his parents – though why that was, he couldn't say. So, just live through it all. Or die . . . He had lived perilously on both his strange journeys.

Try to be practical Like – was one of the soldiers standing near the plane – at the end – was one of those men the ubiquitous stranger from Culver Wood? Who were the elderly soldiers, anyway, commanded by a brigadier in a Rolls Royce? With no weapons that he'd seen except a shotgun . . . Ah, wait a minute, though. There was a volunteer army called the Home Guard, wasn't there? Kind of like the Territorials. In the Second World War. Like the militia he had seen in those earlier times. That would be it. But what did it matter? He no longer had the urge to explore what was happening to him, in terms of finding out about the past. It was too scary. And in this last instance, what could he do, anyway? Ask questions of Mrs Robertson? He'd worry her for nothing, in all likelihood . . . Suppose he had one of those fits, or whatever they were, when he was cycling – and was hit by a car? The mistimed tackle showed just what kind of mess he could land in.

The rain dripped on monotonously. Peter recalled another rainy day when he had taken shelter. The horse-drawn plough on the horizon . . . And he had hardly given it a thought. He felt a dead depression sinking into him, numbing his mind and making him as motionless as a block of stone. Still it rained and rained.

'I think we're going to have to talk about it all.'

The voice was young, quiet and familiar. Peter turned his head. Sitting in the corner was a boy with a limp white cotton hat pulled down over his face, giving the impression he had been asleep. It would seem he had been here for some time, for his grey shirt and dark grey trousers bore no signs of the rain. But Peter had been sure the shelter was empty.

'Don't get scared.' The familiar voice was carefully devoid of emotion. 'Introductions.' The hat was tipped back and the face revealed.

His own face.

It looked tired . . . and at first Peter was overcome with relief the face was not that of the stranger in Culver Wood. Then he was slack-jawed and scared beyond thought.

'Don't get scared.' The voice was low; regretful or sad. 'We'll have to take it slowly. I couldn't think of a better or a fairer way for us to meet.'

'I've had it, haven't I?' Peter's voice was identical to that of the person sitting in the corner. 'I've really gone.'

The stranger lightened his voice encouragingly, though his face – Peter's face – remained sober. 'They weren't Home Guard. Well, not yet – not yet in 1940. They were still known as the Local Defence Volunteers. Or am I wrong?'

'Don't ask me.' It was the tired, adult confidence of the other that impressed Peter; he hardly took in what it was that had actually been said.

'Feeling better? You'll get used to it.'

Peter gagged as he spoke, yet managed to get the words out, 'Oh sure – why not?'

'That's really good. Now we're cooking on gas. That's what they say, isn't it? Have a seat.'

The lack of anything that could be construed as threatening had the effect of calming Peter. He thought about it, but could see no reason why he should not do as the other Peter suggested.

So they were sitting side by side. The other Peter smiled. 'Have we got problems!'

'The same problems?' He tried to be equally jokey and failed. His voice shook.

'Not quite. Shared problems, though. You're fine, by the way – don't worry.'

'I'm an ordinary person – right?' Peter was belligerent: the words leapt out like weapons.

'I didn't say that. Let's just say I'm on your side.'

'A friend?'

'In a way.'

Still it rained. 'What's happening?' Peter asked tentatively. 'Do you know?"

The other Peter took his time over this one, reflecting. In some subtle way he was not Peter at all, and the blunt features they shared did not suit his abstracted air of contemplation. Then, 'You had an idea you'd go to Culver Wood tomorrow, didn't you?'

It seemed only reasonable that the look-alike should be able to know his thoughts. If anything, Peter was momentarily reassured by this. Which was odd in itself. 'Yes.'

The Peter that wasn't stood up. He was friendly and matter of fact. 'OK. We'll go. You'd better get home now, hadn't you?'

Peter got up too, on unsteady legs. He said, 'I'm scared. Who *are* you?'

The smile was incredibly broad. 'I'll see you tomorrow, Peter. We'll be all right. Off you go. Stay as calm as you can; follow your instincts – just be yourself. If you trust me, we'll both be fine. If you trust me.'

'How *can* I trust you?'

The look-alike's reply was so soft as to be sinister. 'Well, if you don't, you really are in trouble.'

Peter's hand found the handlebars of his bicycle. He wrenched the machine round and pulled it out into the rain. His double sat back in the corner of the shelter, looking concerned and holding up his hands to show Peter he meant no harm.

Peter's foot slipped from the wet pedal and he and the bike nearly crashed to the ground. Then he was standing on the pedals, and accelerating away from the stuffy shelter, delivered into the open air and the gusting rain, which slapped against his face with stinging force.

After a hundred metres or so he looked back. There was no one on the road and the bus shelter appeared as commonplace as it always had. While glancing back over his shoulder, he unwittingly veered towards the right-hand side of the road and corrected his direction as a car shot by, hooting at him. He heard it sweep back along the road, past the shelter, as he forced the old bike to carry him home at its best pace.

By the time he reached his house the rain had just about stopped and was already lifting itself off the roads in a haze of evaporation.

His mother was in the scrubby garden at the front of the house, struggling with a mass of honeysuckle which the downpour had beaten from the sagging garden fence at the side of the house.

'You're back early,' she panted.

'I got sent off.'

'Oh – that's bad, isn't it? Give us a hand. This stuff's got a life of its own.'

Together they pulled and heaved at the tangled honeysuckle until the bulk of it lay on the top of the fence like a huge, crouching cat.

His mother stepped back and looked doubtfully at their handiwork. 'Well. It looks *better*, doesn't it?' She added vaguely, 'I expect it'll find its own way . . . Sent off, were you? That's not good, is it?' She seemed proud of this proof of her limited knowledge of sport.

'It was an accident.'

'Oh yes, I'm sure. They had to blame *someone*, I suppose. Never mind. Worse things happen at sea.'

Peter was profoundly grateful for her lack of interest. He followed her into the kitchen, where she washed her hands in the sink, briskly, as though she had just come out of the operating theatre in a hospital.

She dried her hands on a tea towel. 'Oh – wonderful news. Your father's been promoted!'

'Has he?'

'Area manager, he's called, now. He's an area manager again! He called. he says he won't actually have anyone working under him, but it show's they've got confidence in him. That's good, isn't it?'

'Sounds great.' It was hard to get enthusiastic about the ups and downs of his father's business life, especially today.

'He's going to take us out one night next week.'

'Oh?'

'A proper dinner. Probably a steak house. It'll be nice, won't it?'

'Great.'

'Smashing, not to have to cook.'

'Oh yeah – all those twelve course meals we get.' It was a weary joke but his mother would be expecting something of the sort from him. *Act natural. Lie if you have to. Tell your troubles to no one.*

His mother giggled. 'Oh, get away. What's on the telly, then?' She picked up the local newspaper. Peter went upstairs.

He had to pass the bathroom to get to his room. The door was open and he saw the mirror. Naturally it had not yet been replaced. He went into the room and stood in front of the mirror exactly as he had on the day it broke. The triangular remnant of glass cut off his face across and down diagonally, so that one eye and the side of his head were missing. His one visible eye looked back at him in solitary desperation. Nothing happened.

When Isobel got back, her father was out on the lawn in a deckchair, reading the manuscript of his own book.

'Good game, was it? Worth getting wet for?'

'Yes, it was, actually. Quite exciting.'

'Who won?'

'We did. Three-two.'

'Peter get one?'
'No. He got sent off.'
'Really?'
'Yes. It kind of turned the game. That's what everyone said. We only had ten men, though, for most of the time. They were jolly good.'
'That happens sometimes.' The Professor was knowledgeable, as always. 'The backs-to-the-wall, spirit-in-adversity syndrome. That's what kept us going in the war.'
'Oh yes? And what did you do in the war, then?'
'I wasn't even a baby, as you very well know.'
'Yes. I bet when you were one, you were a ghastly baby.'
He responded to her good humour. 'You were a very good baby.'
Isobel immediately spotted that he could work an opening here to start criticizing again and wheeled her bicycle past him.
He called after her, 'There's tea on the table. What was he sent off for?'
She stopped and lied. 'Nothing. It was ridiculous. He's probably coming over tomorrow.'
The Professor's mouth tightened. 'Oh. Is he?'

He was tired. He was often tired these days. Yet now it was midnight and still Peter had not slept. He was wondering why he didn't feel frightened. But the truth was, you couldn't be afraid all the time. Just as you couldn't love, or even hate, another person during your every waking moment. Your mind had other things to do.
*Trust me.* He had, for a moment or two. But perhaps the last person one should trust would be someone who looked like you in every detail. It was

confusing, trying to sort things out when you were only half awake . . . If he chose to look at it in a certain light, then he, Peter, might consider himself at least partially responsible for Mrs Robertson's injuries and, by implication, the empty life she seemed to have had since.

He was very close to sleep now, as he turned his thoughts again to the idea of reincarnation . . . coming back to life, over the years, as different people, and living again . . . and dying. Time after time . . . It must be very . . . tiring.

Suddenly he sat bolt upright in bed. A torch. He would need his torch tomorrow. It was in his chest of drawers. He got out of bed, opened the bottom drawer and took out the torch. He'd put it under his pillow in case he forgot about it. He re-inserted himself under the duvet but stayed sitting up, turning the torch over in his hands. He needed this for tomorrow, when he and Isobel would be back in Culver Wood. He would certainly take Isobel, if only because he felt sure the other Peter would not make his threatened reappearance with her around. It was undeniably true he liked Isobel. She wouldn't get hurt, he was sure. Peter lay back, still holding the torch, and thought about Isobel and why it was one liked one individual more than another.

Then he thought: *We're going to be there in daylight. Why would I take a torch?*

# Eleven

And a broom handle.

Isobel saw it tied on to Peter's bike like a second crossbar, running from the underside of the saddle up and out over the handlebars.

'What's that for?'

'You'll see. We're going to the wood.'

'Are we? You never said.'

'That's right – I didn't.'

Evidently Peter was in a positive mood this morning. To Mr Stanton's mute fury, he had arrived shortly after breakfast and had almost at once marched Isobel out of the house for a bike ride.

She was wearing a T-shirt and jeans, as was Peter, and felt very aware of herself today; self-conscious. She moved awkwardly as she mounted her bike outside the garden gate, although she doubted Peter was paying her any special attention.

They set off together down the lane, riding side by side whenever it looked safe to do so. Isobel didn't want to talk about Culver Wood; she sensed Peter would only get cross if she said she didn't want to go. She said, 'I suppose someone told you about the game, then.'

'No, not yet.' He didn't strike her as being even remotely interested.

'Oh, well . . . we won.'

'Oh yes?'

'Yes.'
'That's good.'
They rode on.
'Patel said you should get a meal.'
'Nice of him.'
'But I think you're going to be in big trouble, you know.'
'How was the bloke I clattered into?'
'He could hardly walk, actually. I think he was taken to a doctor after the game.'
'Oh well. He survived, anyway.'
'I mean it, Peter – about being in trouble. People were talking about making an example of you.'
'Nothing for *you* to worry about.'
'Well, I do.' She left a gap for that to sink in. 'Three-two. That was the score.'
'Oh? I always like three-two. A five-goal game's usually a good one. Still, I hope he's all right, anyway. He's a really good footballer.'
It was as if Peter had played no part in the injury incident, or even in the match itself. Well, thought Isobel, he probably wouldn't want to talk about it much anyway, when you thought about it.
He looked across to her and smiled as though he had read her mind. 'It's really hot today.'
'Yes. Great.'
His mention of the weather killed off their conversation.
They had almost reached the wood by the time Isobel spoke again. The longer she had kept quiet the more urgent had grown her need to speak, until she felt that if they didn't talk now, it would be too late.
'Why are we doing this?'
'What do you mean, exactly?'

'Why do we have to go digging around in Culver Wood?'

' "Because it's there." That's what they say about climbing mountains. Why you climb one.'

'Supposing I said I didn't want to?'

'I'd say you didn't have to, then.'

But she was conscious of him becoming inwardly still as he spoke, and knew that he wanted her with him. That decided her. 'It doesn't worry me, what we do.'

'Anyway, it's daytime,' Peter said nonchalantly. 'Race you!'

With a head start he beat Isobel over the last fifty metres to the old wood. He was already standing by his bike when she caught up, laughing. 'I'll get you next time.'

He paid no attention to this. He was making up his mind about something.

'We'll bung the bikes in the wood this time.'

'Oh – why?'

'I just don't like the idea of that man coming across them. He saw where we left them last time.'

'You're crazy – he won't be anywhere near here. It's a million to one chance.'

'We'll still leave them in the wood.'

They manhandled the bikes over the barbed wire and joined them on the other side. Peter said, 'We'll dump them some way in, where they can't be seen.'

His insistence on these precautions began to strike chimes of doubt in Isobel, but he was already some way ahead of her, carrying his bicycle at hip height, and she found herself following without argument, although it wasn't always easy going, with the great roots of the beech trees spread wide and everywhere clutching into the ground with massive tenacity. It was only when Isobel tripped and fell that Peter stopped.

'You all right? Sorry. This is far enough, anyway.' He disentangled her legs from her bicycle. 'The bike's all right. Are you?'

'Yes. I'm all right.'

He bent down and took her upper arms and lifted her to her feet.

Still holding her, he smiled. 'You're the kind of person I like. The kind that doesn't make a fuss.' Then he let go and went back to his own bike to untie the broom handle.

'Perhaps now you'll tell me what that's for,' Isobel said.

'Ah – well – wait . . .' He finished untying the stick of wood and opened his saddle-bag. 'There's this, too.'

'A torch. 'Go on, then – tell me. Isobel was smiling now.

He tossed the torch over to her. 'Catch.' Leaning on the broom handle in the depths of Culver Wood he looked quite at home. 'It's pretty simple. *If* we heard people that night, we certainly never got a sight of them. *If* there's some kind of old temple here, well it's certainly not visible, is it? I've been all over this place over the last year and there's not even a single block of stone – anywhere. With me so far?'

'Go on, then.'

'So, *if* there's any kind of hiding place of any sort, temple or not, it must be . . .'

'. . . Underground.' Isobel was instantly acutely uneasy.

'Yeah. That's it.' He raised the broom handle like a weapon. 'I like this place. I'm not going to be frightened by it.'

'What do you really expect to find?'

That made him think. 'Nothing.' Yet the pause before he spoke contradicted the word when it came.

'And what's the stick for?'

'It *is* a bit stupid, I suppose. I thought I'd bang it around on the ground. Because if there's a cave or a shaft or anything, well it's got to be hollow somewhere, hasn't it?'

The notion of Peter walking around the wood banging down a broom handle struck Isobel as rather more than amusing. He was angry.

'All right – you laugh. It's better than you being scared, at any rate.'

'It'll take *days*.'

'I said we wouldn't find anything, didn't I?' He swivelled away from her and Isobel tagged after him, all her fears dissipated in gleeful anticipation of watching him make a fool of himself. At this moment, as she suppressed the urge to giggle, the imposing beech trees all around them and reaching far above them to push out the sun, were just a collection of tall trees – now no longer frightening.

Peter seemed very undecided as to where to begin his broom stick routine; he wandered onwards aimlessly for quite some time. Isobel became impatient for him to start, because the sooner he started the sooner he would give up.

When eventually he stopped, she thought it was possible he was fed up with looking and had settled on this small clearing as being as likely a spot as they would come across. Perhaps he simply wanted to get started before the resolve left him. She saw that the serpentine root of one of the trees offered a seat and took it. Peter turned to give Isobel a defiant glare and then slammed the broom handle down on the ground, jarring his hands. The stick made only a soft thud on impact, going through the carpet of leaf mould, twigs and earth.

Isobel fought to keep herself from laughing. At random, Peter punched the broomstick down again and again, with the same savage resentment and the same pathetically soft-sounding results. One could see his chagrin building with every blow.

The sounds did not change: it was something more unexpected that caused Isobel to say, 'Wait a minute.'

'Yes – silly, isn't it? I'm stupid.'

'No – I felt something.'

'I didn't hear anything.'

'I didn't say it sounded any different; I said I *felt* something. Something like a tremor in the ground. No – a vibration. Under my feet.'

'So?'

'Well, I thought you'd like to know.'

Peter turned the broom handle in his hands, uncertain if Isobel was trying to make a fool of him.

'Where did I hit when you felt this . . . whatever you felt?'

'It was about three back. Yes – about there, maybe.'

'There?' Thump.

'No.'

'There?' Thump.

'No.'

'There?' Thump.

'Yes. I felt it again.'

Peter got down on his hands and knees and scraped away the topsoil with his fingers. He said, 'Stay where you are. No, do what I'm doing. We'll meet in the middle.'

Isobel set down the torch and crouched to imitate

Peter, working in a slapdash way because she felt ridiculous.

'This is silly.' They inched towards each other.

Despite her lack of care, it was Isobel who found the stone slab. Her scrabbling fingertips encountered a dense, sandpapery surface beneath the earth and she stared up with her hands buried in the earth.

'This is silly. I've found something.'

'Let's have a look.'

'But it's silly – we've only just started looking.' Her hands remained on the stone as if it might move at any minute and she would hold it down.

Peter knelt beside her. He looked frightened, Isobel saw, and she stood up and backed away.

'What's the matter?' he asked with an assumption of surprise that only communicated more fear.

'Let's forget it. Or tell my father or something.'

'You're joking. The whole idea was to find something ourselves.'

It had never actually been stated before, but it was irrefutable. Without further words Peter pressed home his advantage by busying himself with the patch of ground Isobel had left. He cleared the ground with tearing movements of his clawed hands.

Uncovered, the slab was a brownish-grey oval of stone, about a metre in length. Peter tried to dig his fingers under the rim of the slab, to lift it. He could not get his fingers deep enough into the ground. He saw that his nails were torn and already bleeding, as he brushed away from the stone the remnants of leaf mould and dirt that had disguised it. Now he found the secret: at one end of the oval there were three holes bored into the stone, for fingerholds. He cleared these of earth and sunk his fingers into them as if the slab was a flattened ten-pin bowling ball. The stone was astonishingly light, shaped from pumice-stone, it seemed.

Peter and Isobel heard loose earth fall a short distance down the hole left by the removal of the stone. Peter carried the stone door to Isobel and put it down. 'Give me the torch, then.'

'It's over there.'

He went and picked it up. 'Come on.'

'No thanks.'

They stared at each other. Isobel looked vulnerable and distressed; Peter was composed.

'Wait for me, then?'

'Yes.'

'All right.' He gave her a half smile and switched on the torch. 'At least have a look.'

'No. I don't think I will.'

Peter went down on one knee, shining the torch into the cavity. She saw him adopt the position of a sprinter at the start of a race, with his hands on either side of the hole; then he put his feet together and slid down and out of sight in one fluid movement.

He had seen steps, but had elected to take the plunge and get well in before his nerve failed him. Now he was standing in a narrow shaft with the daylight only a metre or so above his head. Below his feet he could see four more stone steps, rounded with age. The shaft opened out at the level of his waist. Going upwards, the steps dwindled into tiny ledges: he had landed on the first step that had the semblance of any real size. Keeping his free hand against the rock wall at his side, he shone his torch on his feet and watched them carry him down. To avoid banging his head he had to lean backwards, much as though he was coming face-forward down a ladder. It would have been easier to go down on his hands and knees, facing the steps, but the idea of turning his back on whatever waited below did not appeal to him. As his feet reached the bottom of the steps, his head was released from the narrow stairwell and he slowly raised the torch to see where he was.

His first sensation was one of surprise, because the underground cavern was so small. The ceiling was almost exactly as tall as he, and roofed an octagonal chamber not very much bigger than the kitchen at home.

The rock walls were marvellously smooth, though cut into them on several sides were deep recesses, which Peter guessed had once held statues. On the eighth wall, facing him, was the glory of the cavern: a picture delicately carved in relief. Peter could only make out the subject as he would a jigsaw, for he had to move the torch light to view it, piece by piece.

In the centre an almost naked man was wrestling a bull to its knees, with a dagger at its throat. The artist had the man's head turned away, preferring to gain his effect by the fear portrayed in the bull's face: fear and wonderment at the power of the man. But of course it wasn't a man, it was a god . . . The two attendants of Mithras flanked the central scene, carrying their torches – the mournful Cautopates and his triumphant companion, Cautes.

Peter passed the torch across the relief several times before he thought to look at the ceiling to see if there were further wonders. It was a disappointment to find the roof was flat and unadorned. He swept the torch beam downwards again and on its way it glanced across a human face.

Someone was watching him from one of the recesses in the walls.

Peter re-directed the beam of light. It was his double, dressed as before in those neutral colours. The boy spoke.

'So the Professor was right, wasn't he? An amazing man, in his intuition.'

Peter surprised himself with his own composure. 'I didn't want him to find this, did I?'

'Not you. It wasn't *you* who didn't want him to find it. It was me. It's been me all along.' The second Peter moved out of his alcove and looked at the picture on the wall. 'We came here just after a local purge of the followers of Mithras,' he said reflectively. 'More than fifteen hundred years ago. His devotees died without giving anything away and it became our secret. It seemed an ideal base at the time. This part of Culver Wood always had sacred, untouchable associations. Perfect in every way for our needs.'

'*Base*? "Our secret"?'

'Mine and the man you were so worried about.' He smiled wryly. 'Personally, I'd be quite happy for the Professor to make his great discovery. But you see, there's another secret here, one that goes deeper – literally. That's the one that's important to you and me. Still, if I'm right in what I expect to find, there's just a chance we can save this upper chamber for your Professor.'

*Upper chamber*. There was another cavern beneath this one, then . . . As though he had known its whereabouts all the time, Peter's torch was at once pointing down to a circle in the floor. In the circle were set three finger-holes. Peter was crouching down and lifting this second lightweight slab almost before he knew it. Immediately he saw a deep red glow coming from far beneath him and inhaled metallic, bitter fumes which almost choked him.

The look-alike sounded worried. 'This is bad. We won't get down to the operations centre now. It's destroying itself. I didn't think it would have reached this stage. Put back the stone, Peter.'

The tension in his voice frightened Peter and as he fumbled the slab back into place he lost his balance and sat down with a thud on the floor of the chamber.

The other Peter was grim. 'Out. Get out. We're too late.' He raised a finger, pointing at the relief on the wall. There was now a long crack running down the picture, splitting the back of the god. As he watched, Peter saw a series of smaller cracks opening up around the original fissure in the rock, like veins bursting around an artery. Then it seemed the whole picture just slid from the wall in a cloud of dust.

'Get out, Peter. Quickly! We're too late.'

Peter rose to his feet, hearing a section of rock drop down beside him from the roof of the chamber.

The whole place was crumbling like rotten plaster.

Peter tried to speak, but his mouth was full of rock dust. There were further, weightier falls of rock. He had lost track of where the other Peter was but could still hear him calling, 'Get out. Get out.'

Staggering to the patch of light by the stairs that led back up into the wood, Peter was sure they would be buried. He heard and felt a rumbling at his back as his hands and feet found the steps, which gave under his weight like dirty sugar cubes. He could hardly see for the dust in his eyes, and it was fortune that guided his feet to enough footholds and his hands to the thin, wayward root by which he could haul himself up and out of the underground dissolution.

He reeled away as the ground behind him caved in with a great sigh.

* * *

Only seconds later it didn't look much. The dust was already settling on an undramatic, irregular depression some two metres deep at its lowest point. When the air was clear again one might imagine it had been there for years.

'I ran away.' Isobel's voice. He turned. 'I thought you'd be killed. I saw the ground shaking – I didn't know what was going to happen.'

'It doesn't matter.' Where was his double now? Buried somewhere in that mess of earth?

Isobel touched his elbow. 'Are you all right?'

'Yes.'

'Was it a temple?'

'No.' He couldn't tell her. Not now. 'I don't know what it was. There wasn't anything down there. It was just a cave.' He wished he hadn't brought her.

'What happened?'

'I don't know. Perhaps I did it somehow – I don't know.'

'I'd better not tell my father. He'd be really angry.'

'It wasn't a temple.'

'He'd still be angry. I just couldn't tell him.'

'No one's asking you to, are they?'

Peter walked away from the sunken ground and stopped when he saw a human shape moving in the trees some distance away.

'Isobel?'

'Yes?'

'Can you get back to the bikes from here?'

'I'm not sure.'

'Try.' He was certain Isobel would come to no harm.

'Aren't you coming?'

'No. Go on.' He pointed to the right. 'It's that way. I'll see you later.'

'Why can't we go together?'

'Because I say so.'

'Oh, that's nice. I was so worried for you.' She felt guilty and ashamed that she'd run away.

'And because you'll do as I ask.' His gaze was neither friendly nor unfriendly. 'You will, won't you?'

'Why should I?' She felt her bottom lip trembling. He continued to look at her in that colourless way and she remembered how the two sports masters had been discomfited by his stare. Trying to be flippant, she said, 'All right. Whatever you say. Happy now?'

'Go on, then, if you're going.'

'All right – I will, then.'

She was upset. Peter watched her go. She walked at first; then she was running. He'd hurt her feelings. Well, that was too bad. At least she would be all right now she was no longer with him. He waited until she was out of sight in the trees and then picked out the tree where he had seen the human form. He walked towards it, passing amongst the muscled trunks of the beeches which had once seemed so peaceful and welcoming. He stopped some metres short of the tree he had targeted.

'All right. Come out.'

The figure came round from behind the tree trunk: his double, the other Peter, looking sympathetic.

'It's a shame. He'd been gone too long. By the time we got there the process was irreversible. A terrible act of vandalism, really – but our secret is safe – yours and mine.' Peter said nothing. 'It's an extraordinary sight, isn't it – that rapid erosion. It's a method by which a centre of operations conceals itself when it's no longer needed. There'll be nothing to find. Now, no one will ever know.'

Peter waited, willing the look-alike to go on. He did, once more reading Peter's thoughts.

'No – I'm not buried back there . . . because . . .' He stepped towards Peter, who stood his ground. The person that was not Peter pointed his finger at a spot between Peter's eyes. 'Because I'm in there.'

Peter backed away from the pointing finger. The other Peter let his hand fall.

Peter swung away and ran in the direction Isobel had taken.

The other Peter stepped out from behind a tree in front of him.

Peter veered to the left and ran faster. The other Peter was again blocking his path.

Peter turned on the spot and his double was still in front of him.

'No more running. I'm here like this – in this form – so that you can understand the idea: you're sharing your life with someone else who is you and yet not you. Think of me as a parasite, if you like.'

The wood was as still and quiet as any church. The two Peters faced one another; one terrified, the other kind. To Peter, the compassion was the most horrifying element of all.

'I'm a being – an organism – that watches. I'm part of you, but a distinct entity too. You could say I was an anthropologist. Or even an archaeologist. You can put any name to it you want, but I call myself an onlooker. What's the expression? "A harmless onlooker."' Peter looked away from him, thinking of running off. 'Stay where you are. We haven't much time.'

Peter found his voice. 'You still haven't told me who the other man was.'

'A scientist. And also a guardian. I monitor life at

first hand; he monitors our environment. As a guardian he's here to monitor me, too, to a limited extent.'

'I don't understand . . .' Peter's head was hurting.

'You're only the last in a line of people to whom I've been a companion. The difference is that after I joined you certain barriers failed to work as they should. So, instead of being a parasite, I've become a part of you. The guardian knew this when you started coming here all the time.'

Wordlessly, Peter started to shake his head, but the other continued lightly, 'Eventually he saw there was no choice and transmitted his final message from the cavern – that night when you came here with Isobel. A guardian isn't required to have much of a conscience, but he was kind enough to come and warn us that it was over. At last.'

Peter tried to get angry. 'None of this is true.'

The second Peter kept his patience in place, and said coolly, 'It's odd, telling you things you know yourself – somewhere. Can *you* think of a better way to research a species than to be *of* them over a few centuries? To grow with them as individuals, feel what they feel over the years as their race develops – or fails to develop? But obviously, the research is invalidated if one's presence becomes active instead of passive. The whole study had to have method, if it's to be scientific. Hence the need for a constant base – which in this case was Culver Wood. No matter where my host eventually lives or dies, I return to this starting point. In that way, you see, it's not just a random survey. Do you see?'

The reasonable way in which he delivered this explanation made it the more grotesque. Peter began to walk, uncaring as to which direction he took. He walked slowly as yet and his alter ego kept pace with him at his side.

Peter said, 'It doesn't sound very scientific to me. This way you'd only know about England – and everyone says we don't count much these days.'

The other Peter was sunny. 'Ah, well, that presupposes there's only one parasite, doesn't it? Though in fact there's need for very few. Well – not many . . .'

Peter was walking slightly faster now. 'Couldn't I just ask you to go?'

'That's very polite. But, no, you can't. We're inextricably linked – we always have been. Or do you think you can break mirrors just by the power of your own personality? Think about it.'

Peter started to walk a little faster still. The speed at which his companion spoke increased in proportion.

'Why do you think you kept coming back here? Why have you been falling back in time? Those aren't your memories – they're mine. Or should I say, "ours"?'

'I don't believe you!' They were walking very fast and his other self became yet more urgent.

'I'm sorry, but you're very special. Every now and then people are afraid of you. Why should they be? Who do you think sent Isobel away just now – you or me? Who do you think brought a torch today?' Suddenly he sounded angry. 'And just what do you think is going to happen to you when I'm recalled – when I go? *What do you think is going to happen then?* You must listen to me. You must trust me.'

Peter broke into a run. The other Peter did not follow, but Peter could hear him calling. 'There's no time left, Peter. We don't have time to argue.'

Peter's shoulder crashed into a tree: he was knocked

off course and went on running in a different direction, slipping, feeling the earth scattering under his feet. He ran without thought or purpose through the everychanging, dappled light of the green wood, until there were no more trees to run through.

He had arrived at the fence to Mrs Robertson's garden. Under the hot sun the scene was one of civilized tranquility: the pampered flower beds, the bushes cropped to order, the old lawn running down to the inland cliff . . .

Peter walked the last paces to the fence and climbed it. He walked across the lawn, heading for the land that belonged to the Ministry of Defence. Halfway up to the house, Mrs Robertson sat in her wheelchair on the lawn. The white scarf was around her neck and she wore her dark glasses. Peter looked at her as he passed: she flicked with her hand at a flying insect and he again saw in his mind the little wave Fran had given at the gate to the field, in 1940. The teasing Fran, who became the bizarrely humorous Mrs Robertson. He felt guilty, as if it was all his fault.

The excavations looked as though they were awaiting the installation of some quaint plumbing system. These barren trenches were hard to relate to real people who had existed, moment to moment, in the drama and confusion of their own present time. He was conscious he was about to take another journey into the past, yet felt no fear before the connection snapped in his mind.

The air swirled around him in a light mist of tiny droplets. It was as if he had been transported back to a time when the very atmosphere was richer and more elemental. The evening was neither cold nor warm and it was not unpleasant to feel the mist clinging to his bare arms.

He was waiting at the extremity of an immense forest, through which a rough path had been beaten. Waiting for whom?

It was ever odder this time. He was at least partially aware of the emotions and thoughts of the body he shared. He was . . . sad. Frightened too, a little; but the dominant feeling was one of desolation.

He was tired of waiting. The man he was waiting for was sick; he would take his time on the forest path.

Peter turned away from the trees and strode away over the damp grass. His feet were bare. He was wearing a grubby white linen tunic tied at the waist and reaching down to cover his knees.

To his right, perhaps a quarter of a ile away, was the fort; abandoned but still hugging itself into the cliff with military resolution. Portus Lemanis. Though it was only an outline through the mist, he knew it well: now and later, when it overlooked the Romney Marsh. Squat, solid, built to last; today it would be complete to every last stone.

*More than fifteen hundred years ago.* He had the certain knowledge he had come back to where it had all begun: the onlooker's first experience of human life.

He walked the last few yards to the brink of the rock-tumbled cliff. The sea was a deep, clear green, except where it rose and fell on the boulders below him. He could taste salt in his mouth, and salt air whipped into his face, knotting his hair with its sticky fingers.

# Twelve

Out on the heavy waters of the Channel he could see a short, wooden, top-heavy merchant craft working its way out from the coast, its two huge perpendicular oars sticking straight down into the water from the stern, acting as a tiller while the vessel manoeuvred to fill its single red sail.

A hand grasped his shoulder and transferred weight from its owner, until Peter had to brace his legs to take the pressure.

'I never see a ship without envying those who travel,' the man said in a rasping, accented voice.

It was his father. While he knew this could not be so – that he was once again sharing a part of someone else's life – he could not help but accept the man as being his own father, because he shared the feelings of the boy in whom he existed. Now he identified pity: pity both for his father and for himself when his father was gonE.

'One day we'll see ships of war sailing in,' the man said.

'Roman ships?'

'No. There will be no more Roman ships but the traders. Trade goes on at all time in all weather. Come. We'll sit for a while.'

Peter turned and put his arm around the man's waist, feeling his sharp ribs through the woollen cloak he had worn all this long summer. he looked up at the dying man as they made their way along the cliff to a flat outcrop of rock, watching him wince at every step.

Peter helped the man sit and settled himself beside him. It was difficult to tell how old his father was, for his face was blanched and sunken and old with pain, though his hair was still thick and black.

'I wanted to get away from your mother. I've something to give you.' The ailing soldier opened his fingers and in his sword hand there lay a golden coin bearing the head of the Emperor Theodosius, shining richly on the calloused palm. 'Take it, Take it.'

Peter's own thoughts were: *I know this coin. I found it buried in a field . . . Over one and a half thousand years in the future.*

He picked the heavy coin from his father's hand and felt his despondency increase. His hands were damp; sweat mingled with the mist.

'Keep it safely. You will have a use for it soon.' The man looked out across the Channel. 'I came a great distance to die here. I did not leave with the legions: I am not a Roman. I have made myself a citizen of no country. Death will put me among friends again. So you see, it is nothing to cry over. When I am dead you will place the coin on my tongue for payment to the ferryman. One cannot travel empty-handed. Your mother will see to the rest.'

Peter said, 'You will not die this year. You are strong.'

The man tried to smile. 'The pain is growing. You can go now.'

As the man stood up, Peter saw the knife strapped to his waist. The cloak closed over it: the bone-handled knife with the silver inlay. His father patted him on the back, lightly, with affection. 'Your mother will be waiting. Hurry.'

'Are you not coming?'

'I shall be here for a while.'

Peter walked to the forest path. When he looked back the man was still standing gazing out over the Channel. Peter felt the coin clenched tight in his hand. He turned again and it was as though he had run into an invisible barrier which at once gave way with a clear *crack*.

He was staring into the eyes of his other self. His own eyes. They were back at the dig and he felt ashamed and disgusted with himself. He should never have let it happen – never have led Professor Stanton to the grave. He had wanted to divert him from Culver Wood, and the very method he had chosen was to lead him to the grave of a man who had, in this extraordinary way, been his father . . . who had, presumably, taken his own life on the cliff, unwilling to accept a less dignified departure from his family.

'You don't belong here any more, Peter,' said his alter ego. 'You too are a citizen of no country.'

Yes. It was true. He asked dully, 'What happened to Philip Sadler?'

'He died in the Korean War.' A grimace. 'It was cold there.'

'Oh . . .' Peter fought to take an interest in his own predicament. 'When you say there's not much time, what do you mean?'

'I mean that I'm going to be taken away, but I don't know when. Very soon, anyway. I'm guessing that I've only been given this extension of time so that we can negotiate as we are doing. But they can't leave me here for long, with no back-up. It'll be soon.'

They began to walk from the archaeological site to the verge of the old cliff.

'When I go back in time I'm always about my own age, aren't I?'

'That's one connection. Another is that there's always an invasion threatening, isn't there? In a way, I suppose it's a reflection of a truth which part of you has suspected for years: that you yourself have been invaded. By me. I'm very sorry about it, if it helps to know that.'

The courteous regrets expressed by his other half made Peter laugh, which surprised him. 'You're quite something, aren't you?'

The other Peter grinned companionably. 'Yes – I am. You'd better hear the worst of it now.'

They came to a stop, surveying the Romney Marsh beneath their feet. The usual sheep grazed and the sun shone down on the fields and farms and the Channel far beyond them.

'The worst of it?'

'They're going to take me. It's a fact. I'll be taken out of you.'

'And?'

'You won't survive it,' he said flatly. 'We're one being now.'

'No. We're talking – we're two people.'

'Because I have to communicate with you on a level that's fair to you. You must believe what I'm telling you. Even if you don't trust me, you must believe me.'

'I'm still *me*, though. I know I am.'

'No – actually you're me. Put your hand on the ground.'

Peter looked at him, then knelt down and did as he was asked. He looked up at the other Peter, whose expression was serious.

'What now?' Peter said.

'Have a look.'

Peter looked down at his hand. There was a dark, acrid smoke coming from between his fingers. Afraid of being burnt, he lifted his hand quickly. The grass had scorched down to the soil beneath. He saw the black, smoking imprint of his hand, which was itself untouched.

'You're me. You already have abilities of which you know nothing. But when I *leave* . . .' The other Peter shook his head. Then he crouched down beside Peter. 'Do you see it now? I'm a part of you. Without me, you cease to exist. The ugly truth is, your only chance of survival is to agree to something you couldn't possibly understand the consequences of. But I offer you the choice anyway, because I'm not here to do harm.'

'What you mean is . . .'

'You could say it just as well as I could. *Think*. The choice is that you agree to become a part of me, wholly, and then I can take you with me. But you'd always be me; you'd never be Peter Ford again.'

'I don't want to be anyone else. I never wanted to be anyone else but me.'

'No. I know. But that is exactly what you would be. *Exactly*. You'd be someone else – a part of someone else's personality, if you like. You wouldn't feel the same, or think the same, but you'd be alive – you'd be there as a part of me. You'd still exist. It has to be your decision.'

It was such a large proposition to take in.

'All right. I'll think about it,' Peter said at last in a low voice.

'Good. Be quick, though.' And he was gone as if he had never been there.

'Pork. Lovely. Where's Peter?'

'I don't know, love.'

'Well, we'll start anyway, shall we? He can have his cold.'

'It's not like him to miss a meal.'

'Ah, well, but he's got a girlfriend now, hasn't he?'

Mr and Mrs Ford knew their son. He would soon turn up, full of lame excuses for his absence.

The Professor and Isobel ate one of those meals that silence makes tasteless. They too were in their kitchen, picking through a beef salad. The sounds of their knives and forks were magnified in the quiet.

'I suppose it's no use suggesting we do something after lunch?'

'Aren't you working, then?'

'Not necessarily.'

'No, thanks anyway.'

Peter was walking back across Mrs Robertson's lawn. She had left, or been taken from, the garden; but even had she still been there, he would not have been aware of her presence. He moved in a straight line, going back directly to the recently created hollow in Culver Wood.

Strangely, it was the thought that he wouldn't be going to the restaurant next week, to celebrate his father's vague 'promotion', that was at the centre of his attention. His father would order wine and then pass unfavourable comment on it while his mother defended the restaurant right down to the stained table cloth, because she was here for a good time and nothing must spoil it. He could see it all. His father would get expansive and start talking about Peter's future and what he should be doing with his life. Eventually they would leave, feeling close,the family bonds strengthened by the treat, and his mother would be smiling and flustered and would complain his father had left too big a tip, and his father would say 'You only live once.'

He passed through the giant trees and saw the other Peter waiting in the patch of sunken ground that was now a part of the wood.

The earth had not yet settled fully and Peter came down into the hollow in a small avalanche of debris.

'Careful,' said his other self mildly. 'How are you doing.'

'Do I have to tell you? Don't you know?'

The Peter dressed in shades of grey made no reply.

'You can't ask me to decide like this,' Peter said firmly.

'It's the rules, you could say.'

'It isn't right.'

'Sorry.'

'I'd like to see my parents.'

'Sorry. I can't let you – not now.'

'Can you stop me?'

'Yes.'

'I don't want to hurt them. They'd be . . .'

'They're going to be hurt whatever happens. There's no magic solution to that.'

'I would like to see them, though. I wouldn't say anything about . . . this.'

'Wouldn't you?' Sure about that? And how would it help, to see them, anyway? It couldn't serve any good purpose; it wouldn't benefit anyone. Believe me, they'll survive. People do. They're designed to survive.'

'But not me.'

'No, Not any more. Keep thinking. It'd be best if you could come to a decision.'

They sat in silence like old friends for whom the need to talk is minimal because they understand each other.

'I don't know. Kids today. I'd have got a thick ear if I missed a meal with the family.'

Mrs Ford was surprised. 'Would you?'

'Well, I'd have got a good talking to.'

'Your dad would'n't say boo to a goose.'

'Well he wouldn't have said much, perhaps – but he wouldn't have liked it.'

'No . . .' She changed the subject. 'Do you think he'll eat cold peas?'

'He'll eat what he's given and that's that.'

Mrs Ford got up. 'I'll phone that girl's father, I think.'

'They won't be in the book.'

'Well, Peter must have the number somewhere. I'll have a look.

'I'll take you for a drive later.'

'I should do the garden.'

'Suit yourself.'

Mrs Ford went upstairs to Peter's room. He had always been a tidy boy, to her continuing astonishment. The room was cell-like to her eyes: hardly lived in. A bed, a wardrobe, a chest of drawers. The bare essentials and a self-assembly desk unit which also served as a bedside table. The bed had been made. It was as if it were a guest room and their guest had been anxious to be no bother to them. Peter's small address book was by the bedside light. It had one of those Walt Disney dogs on the cover. Which one was it? Goofy? Pluto? Dopey? No – Dopey was a dwarf, wasn't he? Inside, the book held very few phone numbers, though Peter had had it for years.

Isobel Stanton. Right.

Professor Stanton picked up the ringing phone in the hallway.

'Hello. Jim Stanton.'

Isobel was at the top of the stairs, about to go to her room. She waited to see who it was.

'Oh yes – Peter's mother . . . Yes . . . No, no he's not with us.' He lowered the phone and called, 'Isobel!'

She was already coming down the stairs, startling Mr Stanton by her sudden appearance. He put his hand over the mouthpiece of the phone.

'It's Peter's mother. She want to know where Peter is.'

'*I* don't know.'

'Well, you have a word with her, anyway. Hello? Mrs Ford? I'll pass you on to my daughter.' He handed over the phone and stood back.

'Hello?'

'That's Isobel, is it?' Peter's mother sounded nice but ill at ease.

'Yuh.'

'Hello, dear. We were wondering where Peter was.'

'I don't know.'

'We thought he might have had lunch with you.'

Isobel glanced at her father. 'No – he didn't. I saw him this morning, though.'

'Yes, I know.'

'We went for a bike ride.' Isobel improvised for the benefit of both listeners. 'He went on from here when we came back.'

'He was coming home, was he?'

'I don't know what he was going to do.'

'Oh.'

'Sorry.'

'Oh, don't you worry. He'll turn up. He was all right though?'

'Yes, fine.'

'His father thought he might be worried about what happened at the match yesterday.'

'No, I don't think he was,' Isobel answered truthfully.

'Oh well. If you see him could you ask him to call?'

'Yuh – sure.'

'Nice to talk to you.'

'You too. Bye.'

'Bye-bye, then.'

Isobel hung up. Her father folded his arms and said quizzically, 'What do you think of your future mother-in-law, then?'

'I don't think that's particularly funny.'

'No. Sorry.'

Isobel wanted to leave the house and get on her bicycle and go and find Peter, but was reluctant to let her father see her concern. So she wandered into the study, studiously aimless. The act she was putting on only made her the more restless and eager to go. Her father followed her into the room and shut the door behind him, adding to the obstacles in the way of her departures.

'What's up?' he asked.

It was difficult to gauge if the question was general

or specific, so she gave the standard answer covering every possibility.

'Nothing.' She sauntered to his desk and riffled through the pages of the manuscript of his book. 'Do you really think you'll find a temple?'

'No. If I'm honest with myself, I think it's unlikely – wherever I look. But it's the search I enjoy, if you can understand that. There's a saying, "It is better to travel hopefully than to arrive." '

'Seems a bit pointless.' She wondered if she could ever tell him of the discovery Peter and she had made. No. It was a question of loyalty as much as anything else.

'I do get discouraged, actually,' said Mr Stanton. 'From time to time. But then I see my old friends at the window there and I start to think how marvellous it would be if one day I was to come across something really special.'

They both looked at the wooden statues. The painted figures looked at their least lifelike in the bright sunshine beating in from the garden. *Anyway, it wasn't a temple.* Peter had told her that and she had believed him.

'They're just pieces of wood,' Isobel said finally.

'Perhaps.'

'Besides, it's people who are important. Not relics.'

'Do you think I don't know that? But the past forms the future, doesn't it? It's no less important. We're all of us creatures of the past.' They seemed to be in one of the rosier patches of their relationship, so he added, 'I wish I was better with you. You're the person I care about.'

'Well, I've got better things to do than hang about here.' Isobel took a deep breath and made for the door.

Mr Stanton reached the door before her and opened it for her. 'Exit the queen of mystery. Where are you going?'

'Out. I'm bored.'

'You can bring Peter here any time you like, Bella. Do remember that. You can bring any of your friends here – any time you like.'

'Peter's the only friend I've got.'

He said wearily, 'Yes, of course,' and stepped back to let her pass through the doorway.

Standing between the two painted statues, Mr Stanton watched his daughter wheel her bicycle down the garden path. She was very upright. Her whole manner today formed a perfect example of how she had been since Mrs Stanton died. Brittle, remote, ungiving.

On the ride to Culver Wood Isobel let the sun do her thinking for her; the brilliant afternoon allowed no sinister explanation of Peter's absence from home. He was a funny boy, with his own ways. She'd find him and tell him to be more responsible.

The anticipated pleasure of showing Peter how sensible she was diminished as she neared the shadows of the wood, and as she clambered over the barbed wire her mind was seeking out more dramatic reasons for his not going home. Perhaps the floor of the wood had given way elsewhere and he was trapped . . . or suffocated . . .

Finding the bicycle did nothing to allay her worries. She moved further into the wood, starting to call his name – softly, because a louder hail would reveal the beginnings of a panic she would not let herself feel.

'Peter? Peter?

The light, tentative voice had a ghostly effect. For

a second, Peter had the wild idea it was Mrs Robertson – Finaces – youthful again and anxious to renew their relationship. He looked at his alter ego. They had neither moved nor spoken; now the other Peter stood up and tiltted his head, trying to fix the whereabouts of the calling voice.

'Peter?' came the call.

Peter waited passively. His other self frowned, examined his finger nails, and vanished so swiftly, utterly and unexpectedly that Peter started to his feet.

'Peter?'

Definitely Isobel's voice. He was going to call back to her when he felt his feet rise from the ground. He was travelling directly upwards into the air, through the branches of the beech trees. His body still felt heavy; a dead weight propelled by a force heedless of gravity. Leaves fingered his face: he was moving sideways now, coming to rest at the junction of a broad branch and the trunk of one of the trees. He was a good twenty metres above the hollow, which was visible through a succession of branches and leaves. Though he still felt supported by the strength which had lifted him, he held on to the rough bark of the tree, afraid the power would abandon him and he would fall.

Either he had lost the desire to call back to Isobel or it was not permitted; for which ever reason it might be, he had no inclination to open his mouth.

He watched Isobel come into the little clearing. Her body was foreshortened by this high vantage point: he could see only the top of her dark head and her feet when she stopped immediately under him, calling again.

'Peter? Are you still here? Come out if you are. I'm not playing games. You are here, aren't you?'

He saw her find the broom handle, which lay on the ground near the hollow. She picked it up and at once let it fall again, sounding angrier.

'You're not being very fair, Peter Are you here? Where are you?'

It seemed she stood there for an age, listening for any sound that might betray Peter's presence; then in contradiction to her complete immobility she called, 'I'm not looking for you any more. If you can't be bothered with me, I can't be bothered with you.'

She ran off in the direction from which she had come. Peter could hear her every footfall. The rapidity of her departure suggested fear.

Long moments elapsed after the last sound had been devoured by the huge quiet of the wood. Peter relaxed his hold on the tree trunk and was immediately moved out sideways into space and lowered rapidly to the ground as if he were held in a safety harness attached to a crane. The pressure around him fell away.

From behind him the other Peter said, 'We like her, don't we? Do you need to talk any more? I truly don't know how long we've got.'

Peter did not turn around. He knew his double would be standing there again with that expression of deep concern. He put his hands in his pockets and took a few steps away. 'No. Not really. I think I've got it. I'm with you now. There's not much of me left that's really independent of you, anyway, is there?'

'No.'

'And when we think about it, even if there was, you couldn't leave me here, even if I did live. Not now.' No response from behind him. 'You're only asking *me* to decide because it's your policy to interfere as little as possible.'

No response. Peter turned to look at the Peter who didn't exist but who was standing there all the same. 'And if I don't ask where we're going it's because either I know the answer or because I know you're not free to give it. So really there's nothing left to say.'

'So you've made your decision.'

'I still wish I could see my parents.'

'It can't be done. It's sad, I know. I don't want to hurt anyone.'

'That's me talking.'

'Or me. Both of us.'

Neither spoke for several seconds, then the second Peter said, 'Last question. You do know I haven't lied to you?'

'I trust you, if that's what you mean. I believe you and I trust you.'

'Yes, that's what I meant. That's pretty brave.'

The phantom Peter moved into the centre of the hollow. 'I thought we'd give it a measure of ceremony. All right?'

'OK.' Peter's heart was racing. He moved in to join the other Peter.

They faced one another and then, as one being, extened their arms, palms outwards, until they were almost touching.

Peter's other half watched him closely; perhaps waiting for a last minute change of mind.

Then he said, 'Welcome.'

Peter's fingers developed pins and needles and he saw his mirror image, opposite him, explode into a vapour that rushed at Peter's hands with horrifying speed, disappearing without trace or sensation.

The pins and needles left his fingers.

For a moment or two Peter felt no difference at all.

# Thirteen

'Anyone seen Peter Ford? You – Isobel – have you seen him this morning?'

'No, Mr Jarvis.'

'Right. Into the book with him.' Mr Jarvis, Geography, grinned without humour. 'I understand he went into the book on Saturday, too, didn't he? We have a clogger in our midst! A midfield destroyer – isn't that the term?'

There was little laughter from the class and Mr Jarvis looked sour. 'Books out! While the north of Finland has mountainous areas, the south and centre of the country is flat, producing the grain and potatoes that comprise the principal crops of the country. *However*,' he threatened, 'it is the forests of Finland which account for over half its exports. It's no mystery, because forests are made up of trees and trees are made of wood, aren't they?'

'Stay awake, Leadbetter. You are particularly ugly in repose. It may be unrefreshing to be reminded that Denmark also produces great quantities of potatoes and grain, but—'

The classroom door had opened.

'Excuse me, Mr Jarvis.' It was the captain of Saturday's football team.

'Yes, What is it?'

The boy went over to the impatient teacher and spoke in a self-conscious whisper. Mr Jarvis listened without interest.

'Does he? Isobel Stanton, your presence is requested in the headmaster's room. Should you find the time in your conversation with the great man, you might be good enough to mention that your level of attention to work in my class is so minimal as to be non-existent. Go on – hurry up. We collectively promise to do our utmost to survive for a few minutes without your radiant company.'

In the corridor Isobel asked, 'What's up?'

'I don't know. He seemed all right, though. Not aggravated.'

When they reached the door, the football captain knocked, winked at Isobel and went on his way.

'Come in.'

The headmaster, a tiny man with abundant energy, was sitting behind his desk fiddling with the pipe no one had ever seen lit. Beside him stood a St John Ambulance man, whose dark uniform was necessarily of a large size.

'It's about Peter, is it?' Isobel asked, with dramatic premonitions of tragedy.

'Why should you think that?' The headmaster leant forward keenly, like a policeman.

Of course. The other man was a policeman, not an ambulance man. Yes, that was a policeman's uniform. How silly of her.

He was sympathetic in manner, as the ambulance man would have been. He talked unnaturally slowly and clearly. 'If you don't mind, I'll do this. It's Isobel. That's right, isn't it?'

'Yes.'

'Yes, that's right. I'm going to talk to all the boys

and girls in your class, but I thought we would have a word first, you see.'

Sounding apologetic in advance of offending her, he said, 'You and Peter Ford were together yesterday, weren't you?'

'Yes.'

'Yes.'

The policeman congratulted her on her co-operation. 'Yes, that's right . . . You're very good friends, aren't you?'

'Yes. We are.' The words *'Just good friends'* darted into her mind and she nearly smiled. She must be nervous.

'Well, Isobel, the most important thing for you just now is to remember that. You're Peter's friend, so you'll want to help in any way you can, won't you?'

'Of course. What's happened?'

'Well, he's missing. His mum and dad are going through rather a bad time. Do you know anything about it, Isobel? Like where Peter is?'

He was so patient and gentle he ,ight have been talking to a toddler. Isobel felt patronized. 'No. I've no idea. His mother phoned us up a couple of times yesterday, but we couldn't help. I don't know what Peter's up to.'

The big, unintroduced policeman fixed her with his most friendly smile. 'But you're his friend and you're going to help us, aren't you?'

'Yes – I said . . .'

'So you'll tell us all about what you got up to yesterday.'

The two men waited while Isobel quickly worked out how much of the truth she would have to release. If Peter was 'missing', it might well be of his own volition. Her protective instincts rose to the fore.

'What we did was, we went for a bike ride. We do quite often.'

Approval again. 'That's right. Where did you go, exactly?'

'Well actually we were trespassing. We went into Culver Wood. That's over by—'

'I know where it is.'

'We didn't do any harm. We, um, we didn't do anything.'

'So why did you go there?' It was a reasonable question, reasonably put.

'Oh, well – it was Peter's idea, actually. He just kind of likes it there.'

'Does he?'

It did sound odd. 'Yes. So that's why we went.'

'And what happened?'

'I said – nothing happened.'

'You didn't get up to anything in the wood?'

'No – we did not.' Isobel was furious and was suddenly sure she would not tell the policeman about Peter's incursion underground. 'Nothing at all,' she added firmly.

'So what happened, then?'

'You keep saying that – about something happening.'

'Your father has given me permission to interview you, you know.'

Oh, had he just! 'Look, *nothing happened*. Peter got moody so I went home. That's all,'

'Yes? Moody about what?'

'I don't know . . . He had that trouble at the football match the day before . . .'

The headmaster and the policeman exchanged

glances. The policeman went on in the same inhumanly gentle way, 'Yes. We know about that. He was upset about the game, was he?'

This tender interrogation was getting under Isobel's skin. She took the easy route out. 'I think so, yes.'

'Yes, that sounds very probable. You didn't come across anyone else, did you?'

'No.'

'Not at any time?'

'No. We didn't see anyone.'

'A car, for instance?'

'No – I told you.'

'I see.'

But they had on an earlier occasion. And it had been rather alarming. She'd better tell about that, at least. 'We did see a man outside the wood another time. He spoke to us. He was a bit stranger.'

If it were possible, the policeman became even more gentle. 'Oh, yes? Could you tell me about him?'

'It was days ago.'

'All the same . . .'

'He was funny. He spoke in a funny way. It was like he wasn't used to it. Talking. He was – I don't know – Peter thought he was a bit mental.'

'What time of day was this?'

Oh dear. 'Morning. Quite early – We met up for a bike ride before school and we passed the wood and he was walking along the road.'

'What did he look like? Can you remember?'

The headmaster shifted uncomfortably in his chair. These questions fed his worst fears for Peter.

'Well,' Isobel started, 'he wasn't very tall . . .'

'They had a talk with me too, you know. A private one.' Patel said with more than a trace of pride.

'Did they?' Barry Leadbetter knew it already.

'Yes. I couldn't help them.'

It was lunchtime. Together with about a hundred other pupils they watched the white police car drive out of the gates. Isobel sat in the back looking remarkably guilty.

Patel went on, 'She won't be able to help them.'

'How do you know?'

'Look – if Peter was up to anything he'd tell me, wouldn't he? I'm his mate.'

'Oh sure. "I knew the murdered man well, your honour. He was like a brother to me. I'll kill the swine who did this." '

'Ha, ha.'

'What about lunch, then?' Barry said, peering at the legs of one of the senior girls.

'Yes, all right.' They turned to go back into the school. Other sensation-seekers were drifting back, too. Barry and Patel quickened their pace.

'He'll turn up,' Barry said.

'Oh yes. I should think so.'

'He can look after himself, Peter can. You always get that impression – you know?'

'What'll happen is, there'll be a big search up and down and around and he'll turn up and you'll get people shouting about the waste of public money. My dad says it's criminal the way public money is spent.'

'Does he?'

Patel wondered if it was possible that he and Barry would become friends.

The degree to which the police and their helpers took seriously the search for Peter was emphasized by the presence of the German Shepherd dog. He did not appear to be happy to be out and about in Culver Wood on a sunny day; he was a professional, as downbeat in attitude as his handler.

Other than the dog and his poker-faced handler there were two further policemen: the line of searchers was elsewhere made up by members of the archaeological dig in the adjoining field. Brian Vosper had his camera with him.

Isobel was with her father and the policeman who had questioned her, Inspector Lumb. Her father had said little to her since meeting her on the road by the wood, though he had squeezed her arm lovingly. She knew that at some stage he would ask her why she and Peter had been in Culver Wood on Sunday.

'You're sure they were here?' Inspector Lumb asked. Perhaps that's why he had not introduced himself earlier: it was a faintly ridiculous name.

'Pretty sure. I can see them in my mind. His bicycle's really old and battered. Mine looked, well, even newer beside it.'

The Inspector was despondent, as though his hope had been to find the bicycle, then Peter's body, and then go home for tea. 'Never mind. On we go. We'll cover the wood, now we're here.' He raised his voice so that his words carried to the nearest in the line.

Isobel began to feel anxious. Someone would know the wood. Someone would point out that the depression left by the collapse of the underground cave or tunnel had not been there before. They would unearth Peter's torch – or find that silly broom handle – or perhaps they'd come across the oval stone Peter had lifted. She should have told the whole truth right at the start. But now . . .? *Yes, there was something I left out. We were looking for a temple and the ground caved in. I forgot about that.*

Her worries were needless. The hollow had the look of being an age-old, permanent feature. Even where the roots of one of the trees had been exposed there was no tell-tale discolouration to hint at the fact the hollow had only been made the day before. She and her father and the Inspector walked down into the saucer shape of the sunken ground. Beneath the leaf mould and twigs the soil was packed down at the same consistency as the higher ground around them. At once it was hard to remember her horror at the rippling subsidence of the ground, because it couldn't have happened – not here. Peter must have spent hours over this quite brilliant job of invisible mending.

She felt quite confident in saying, 'We sat down here, I remember.'

'And you talked, did you?' Inspector Lumb asked. Mr Stanton put his hand on the back of Isobel's neck in a silent expression of reassurance.

'I suppose we did, yes. But not much. It was a hot day. Then I got bored and went home.'

This was not enough for her father. 'Is that all?'

'Well, Peter wasn't being very nice. He wasn't saying much. He doesn't sometimes.'

'He was upset about the football match,' the Inspector handily reminded her.

'Yes, that's right. I didn't want to talk about it really. He was . . . quite happy to be left alone.'

She led the way out of the hollow.

They were at the point where the wood met the inland cliff. Inspector Lumb pushed his foot under the fence and watched a clod of earth tumble down.

'Dangerous place,' he said non-committally. 'You didn't come here?'

'No.'

'All right, Mr Stanton, Take her home. I'll give you a call if we need her again. Thank you, Isobel. You've been a great help. There's nothing more you can tell us?'

'No, I'm afraid not.'

For the first time he had appeared at ease with her and had talked to her as an equal, and Isobel felt ashamed she had told him so little. Still, it was done now.

'Mr Stanton? I'm Peter's father.'

When Isobel and her father emerged from the wood they found Mr and Mrs Ford were standing beside their small saloon car, which contrasted with the Professor's expensive Range Rover exactly as had the bicycles of their respective children. A police sergeant was with them. Mr Ford took a step towards the Professor, perhaps wondering whether to shake hands.

'We saw you on the telly the other day.'

'Did you?'

'Yes. And this is Isobel, is it?'

'Yes,' said Isobel.

'Hello, dear.' Mrs Ford was a nervous shambles in a skirt and blouse that were too tight for her. Isobel liked her.

Mr Stanton said, 'There's no sign of him there.' He made it sound as though this was hopeful news.

'Well, no, there wouldn't be,' Mr Ford said with forced confidence. 'No – he's off somewhere else, obviously. I'll give him a piece of my mind when he comes trotting home. You feel so silly with all these people put to all this trouble.'

'Still – better safe than sorry,' Mr Stanton said heartily. The phrase did not mean anything but it had an encouraging ring.

'Oh yes!' Mr Ford was equally positive.

'It must be upsetting for you, dear,' Mrs Ford said to Isobel.

'He'll be all right, Mrs Ford.' Yet another piece of spurious confidence.

Peter's mother was not prepared to play the general game. 'Will he?' Her voice quavered with doubt.

'He's pretty practical,' Isobel said.

Mrs Ford swallowed. 'It's nice to know he's got a good friend, anyway. A nice girl.'

Mr Stanton said, 'I must get Isobel home and get some food into her. Please give us a ring if there's anything we can do.'

'Oh certainly,' Mr Ford said, then added vaguely. 'Oh yes, we'll be in touch . . .'

'Goodbye,' Isobel said to Mrs Ford.

'Goodbye, dear.' Mrs Ford wore an unrealistic smile; she was trying to assure Isobel she wasn't really worried.

Isobel saw the effort the smile cost her. It was so hard to keep in place it might have been physically hurting Mrs Ford.

In the Range Rover the Professor accelerated away from Culver Wood. Isobel was looking back at Mrs Ford.

Her father let out a sigh. 'I'm afraid I haven't got a very good feeling about all this.'

'Nor have I.'

'What have you been holding back?' he asked conversationally.

'Nothing.'

'Why do you have a bad feeling about what might have happened to Peter, then?'

They rounded the bend and the wood was gone. Isobel faced front.

'He's unlucky,' she said after a while.

'Is that all?'

She didn't answer.

'Why did you go into the wood in the first place? Why Culver Wood?'

'To annoy you, I suppose.'

'I might have known it.'

'I don't have to tell the police that, do I?'

He sighed again. 'Oh Bella . . . No, of course not. I'm glad you told me, though. Have you got anything else to tell me?'

'There's nothing else to tell.'

He gave her a sidelong glance. 'For instance, Peter didn't say he thought I might be right that there could be something of archaeological interest there?'

'For instance, no'

'He's got a gift, that boy, you know. I'm not too conventional and stupid to see that.'

'As a matter of fact he said there wasn't a temple there. He actually said it out loud.'

Professor Stanton was fascinated. 'Really?'

'Really.'

'Extraordinary . . . But how did he know?'

'You'd have to ask him that.'

'Yes . . . I think you should consider the possibility that something has happened to him, Bella.'

She turned on him furiously. 'What do you know about it?'

'Nothing at all – less than you, I'm sure.'

She calmed down. 'If something has happened, do we have to stay here?'

He thought for a moment. When he spoke again he too was quiet. 'Not if you don't want to.'

And somehow that settled it. Something had happened to Peter. Something awful.

It was that basic and sometimes basest instinct, curiousity, which prompted Isobel's actions that evening. Mingling with an awareness that Culver Wood and only Culver Wood could be at the heart of the mystery of Peter's disappearance, was the childish urge to experience fear. Supporting these motive forces was the improbable understanding that by going to the wood she would be closer to Peter. Nevertheless, she would not have gone if the opportunity had not presented itself.

The phone call Mr Ford had promised Professor Stanton had duly come at six o'clock. An exhaustive search of the upper environs of the old inland cliff had not proved productive. There had been no sightings of Peter or his bicycle anywhere and now there was to be mounted a major search of the lowlands of the Romney Marsh. 'Just thought I'd keep you in the picture.' Once 'in the picture' it was impossible for Mr Stanton not to enlist among the searchers.

Now Isobel had Mrs Davies as a companion for the next few hours. The woman's motherly sympathy had driven her mad within a quarter of an hour, and it was only after the television had worked its hypnotic spell that Mrs Davies stopped looking understanding.

Dusk was creeping down outside and Mrs Davies got up to draw the curtains. It was in a commercial break before the start of an American soap opera about rich people behaving badly.

Mrs Davies came back to the sofa. 'Your father's a

very kind man, isn't he? Going on the search party like that.'

'Mmm.'

'His not being a local man and all. My husband would have gone, if he was alive.'

There was no answer to that.

'Though he wasn't much of a chap for walking. Hated the Marsh, too. So windy.' Mrs Davies pulled her mouth down at the corners in agreement with her dead husband. 'Imagine if it was all still sea there. It would be quite a sight, wouldn't it?'

'Mmm.'

'I'll just turn it up a bit.' Mrs Davies went over to the television and raised the volume on a jingle for a deodorant. Isobel stood up and stretched elaborately.

'I'm tired. I'm going to bed, I think.'

'Are you? Well, I don't blame you. It's been a tiring day for you. Upsetting.'

'Yes.'

'Shall I make you a hot drink before you go?'

It was a reluctant offer, as she was hopelessly addicted to the soap opera.

'No, thanks. Thanks for coming round.'

'My pleasure.'

'See you, then.'

'Sleep well.'

The challenging opening music of the programme rang in Isobel's ears as she closed the door, With that blasting away there was no need to tramp upstairs and then sneak down.

The front door was on the latch, so that was no problem either.

The day was cooling rapidly and colour gradually left the sky with the passing minutes. The twilight was traditionally mournful, conducive to rueful, satisfying thoughts of impermanence.

Isobel was conscious she was riding her bicycle at a speed dictated by the dusk; a pace so stately as to lend a feeling of inevitability to every steady revolution of the wheels. She supposed she could get to like the country, if she stayed. She yawned. It seemed she could travel on like this for hours.

The countryside was being shaded in by a soft lead pencil as Isobel slowly cycled the last yards to Culver Wood. It was only then she realized she should have fought to get here faster. For, if it was increasingly dark on the road, how gloomy would it be in the shadows of the trees?

She dealt with the first stirrings of fear by leaving her bike propped up in full view of the road. It was a form of insurance. The fence was hard to climb, for no reason other than her nerves, and she tore the pocket of her jeans.

By some strange alchemy of nature, the wood was lighter than she had thought it would be, and had retained the heat of the day, as if it operated on its own time scale. Though the air was heavy and sombre she had no difficulty in moving from tree to tree as she followed a path which now seemed very familiar.

There, that was where they had left the bikes. Fine. So . . . just walk on . . .

A wind sprang up and disturbed the youngleaves on the beech trees. The rustling sound was distinctly unpleasant. Unconsciously, Isobel walked faster.

The hollow was a dark basin set into the woodland floor and it drew Isobel like a magnet. She was fairly sure she could get straight back to the road from here, so she wouldn't go any farther. The idea of being lost in Culver Wood was too chilling to contemplate. She sat down in the hollow and listened to the wind feeling its way among the trees, as blind as she would be if she stayed here much longer in the gathering gloom. She did not want to move, though. It was weird. She had left Peter here and he had vanished. Perhaps he had even been murdered – yet she still wanted to stay here, to be where he had been when she had last seen him.

A feeling of great loneliness grew in her. She was telling herself this inner desolation was only a sign that the wood was deserted but for her, when she heard footsteps crushing their way through the trees. She did not hear them from a distance: they were already near at hand. Her stomach fluttered and her heart drove harder.

It could not be Peter because the steps were so heavy.

# Fourteen

It would be a man. Probably a large man. She bent her head down and held her breath, rigid with fear.

A very large man. The earth quivered as he came closer, breaking his way over the ground with slow, pounding steps. Isobel shut her eyes tightly.

'Isobel.'

It was Peter's voice. She could not unlock her body to look up.

'It's only me, Isobel.'

His voice was so normal and so light and friendly that she found she was able to lift her head.

He was smiling. It was a smile suited to the evening light: a slow, regretful, tired smile. 'What are you doing here?'

She stood up on disobedient legs, angry. 'I could ask you that. What do you think you're doing – crashing around and scaring me like that? It's a horrid thing to do.'

'Sorry.'

'You know what you've done, don't you? You've only got half the country looking for you, you know.'

He crouched down carefully and picked up a handful of earth, letting it run through his fingers.

'They'll be looking for you, too, soon,' he said.

'Not if we go straight home – now.'

'Yes, I think you should.'

'And you. You're coming too.'

'No.' It was as final as the word could ever be.

'What are you doing, then – running away or something?'

'Not exactly. I am going away, though.'

'You're taking your time about it.'

He shrugged.

Isobel felt her anger drain out of her. 'You should have told me. I'm on your side. You know that.'

'Yes, I do. I've been very lucky to have you as a friend.'

Why must he sound so sad? Why must it seem the sadness was for her and not for himself?

He mustn't go. 'How can I make you stay? What can I do?'

'There's nothing you can do.'

'I suppose I should feel grateful you're even speaking to me.' Was it her imagination, or was the light growing brighter around them?

He grinned suddenly. 'Actually, I suppose you should, in a way.'

He looked up and Isobel did too. It was quite definitely getting lighter. In all probability there had been cloud cover which was now being hurried away by the wind. In all probability . . .

Isobel said, 'Where's your bike? Why didn't the dog find you? Did you go somewhere else?'

He chose only to answer the last question. 'No. I've always been here.'

'Doing what?'

'Waiting.'

'What for?'

Again he did not answer her question. 'It's very odd . . . that we're here, saying goodbye. I'm glad, though. It's good we got the chance. I'm going to miss you.'

He stood up. In an indefinable way he seemed not only bigger but infinitely more sure of himself. It was now light enough to see his skin had a grey pallor. He must be very tired, Isobel thought, and felt a surge of affection.

She walked across to him. 'Peter . . .'

He was concentrating his attention elsewhere, perhaps listening for something. He said, 'No, Isobel. You go now. I'm staying here, but you have to go. Now.'

'I'm staying too,' she said stubbornly. He reached out and took hold of her upper arm. '*No*.'

His grip was incredibly hard and painful. She touched his hand and did not feel flesh. It was a harder substance by far. The discovery was so very alien to everything she had ever experienced that she could not feel frightened. The light was growing stronger and now she saw it was focused on the area immediately around Peter. She touched his face: it was marble, smooth and impervious.

'Peter . . .' Now it was she who felt pity for him.

'So you can't come, you see.'

'What's happened to you?'

'An accident. Think of it as an accident.'

Isobel was scared for him and whispered, 'It's like you're made of stone. Or rock . . . "Hewn from the living rock",' she quoted fearfully.

'Yes. Perhaps it happened before, somewhere else, a long time ago.' He smiled and his eyes held a sad joke in them. 'It doesn't matter.'

'What happened, though?'

'You must think of it as an accident.' Then he said, 'It's getting brighter.'

It was. Isobel took a step back. Peter was now standing in a distinct shaft of light which grew yet brighter as she watched. He reached forward and touched her forehead with extraordinary gentleness, tracing a line down to her eyebrow. He did not attempt to put words to this gesture, but said softly as his hand drew back, 'Will you walk away a few steps? Just for a minute?'

It was not the kind of command one disobeyed, if only because the action required was so easy. Isobel turned and took one, two, three paces away. She thought, *There must be something I can say. Something to tell him how I feel to have had him as a friend.*

She turned back. 'Peter . . .'

He had vanished. She heard a high singing note in the air. It lasted for perhaps five seconds.

Whatever it was that had happened to Peter, it was ended.

As the note diminished so too did the light, and Isobel was left in the early darkness of a summer night, in a wood that had been Peter's favourite place and where she had failed to say goodbye to him. As she had failed to say goodbye to her mother. She was confused. People went away without warning, when there was so much you should say to them.

She put a hand on the spot where her ribs met her stomach. It was painful. She stayed where she was, rocking her upper body slightly to quieten the pain, and experienced the first intimations of a feeling she had not allowed before: the terrible anxiety of loss.

Professor Stanton was tired as he drove by Culver Wood. he was travelling fast, keen to be home as soon as possible. The lights of the Rnge Rover swept over the sparkling outline of Isobel's racing bicycle. Mr Stanton was braking even before he saw that Isobel stood beside the bicycle with her arms folded and her head down.

The Professor reversed a short way and got out of the car, enraged with worry.

'What the hell are you doing?'

Wordlessly, without surprise, Isobel picked up the bicycle and brought it over to the car. He saw she had been crying.

He said, 'I'm sorry. It was a bit of a shock. You should be at home. What did you think you were doing?'

He opened the back of the car and heaved the bike in without ceremony. 'It's just not on, Bella. A ridiculous trick to play. You were lucky I was passing. It could have been . . . *anyone*.'

He took her round to the passenger door and shoved her up on to the seat. When he was behind the wheel of the car, he left his door open so that the light stayed on in the interior. He was going to tell her in more detail what he thought of her irresponsibility, but she slid right across to him and put her head on his shoulder. He stroked her hair, felt foolish because he had given way so soon, and slammed his door shut.

He did not drive off immediately, but sat holding the wheel and said, 'We didn't find him.'

He let out the clutch and they drove off. Professor Stanton looked at Isobel. In the light from the dashboard he could not be sure what her expression was, but her head was heavy on his shoulder, which suggested she was content to be with him.

'What were you doing?' he asked again when they were nearly home.

This time she responded. 'I just wanted to make sure Peter wasn't there.'

'But he wasn't.'

It was a statement and after a pause she answered with another statement.

'No. He wasn't.'